"I believe," Trobt said, "that you came here to find any weakness we might have in our very selves.

"I think that this may be the *first* Game, and that you are more dangerous than you want us to see, that you are accepting the humiliation of allowing yourself to be thought of as weaker than you are. You intend to find our weakness, and somehow you expect to bring to your worlds what you find."

I looked across at him without expression. "What weakness do you fear I've seen?" I countered.

"You must by this time have the certainty that you will die," Trobt answered. "Yet you persist in acting in ways not consistent with that certainty. Do you believe that we can be outsmarted, even when you are in a position from which there can be no escape?"

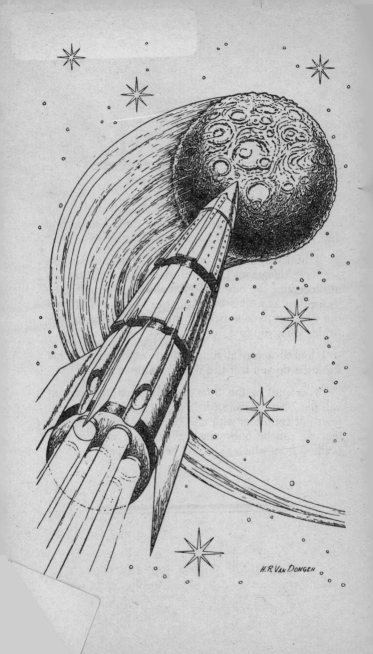

H.R. Van Dongen

SECOND GAME

Charles V. DeVet
and
Katherine MacLean

DAW BOOKS, INC.
DONALD A. WOLLHEIM, PUBLISHER

1633 Broadway, New York, N.Y. 10019

FIRST PRINTING, MAY 1981

1 2 3 4 5 6 7 8 9

DAW TRADEMARK REGISTERED
U.S. PAT. OFF. MARCA
REGISTRADA, HECHO EN U.S.A.

PRINTED IN U.S.A.

1

The sign was big, with black letters that read:

I'LL BEAT YOU THE SECOND GAME

I eased myself into a seat behind the play board, straightened the pitchman's cloak about my shoulders, took a final deep breath—and waited.

A lean Fair of Seasons visitor glanced at my sign as he strolled by. His eyes widened with arrested attention—and anticipated pleasure. He shifted his gaze to me, weighing and measuring me with the glance.

I knew I had him.

He changed direction and came over to where I sat. "Are you giving any odds?" he asked.

"Ten to one," I answered.

"More than generous.". He wrote on a blue slip with a white stylus and dropped it at my elbow. "A dronker," he said, and sat down opposite me.

"We play the first game for feel," I said. "Second game pays."

Gradually I let my body relax, slouching into a half-slump. I could feel my eyelids droop, and the corners of my mouth

5

pulled down. I probably appeared tired and melancholy. Or like a man operating in a gravity heavier than normal for him.

Which I was.

I had come to this alien world named Veldq two weeks earlier. My job was to learn why its humanoid inhabitants refused all contact with the Federation.

During the past several centuries Earth's colonies, and colonies of colonies, had expanded across the spiral arm of their galaxy until they encompassed seven light-years of space. If you studied a star chart our territory would seem to encompass a mere few inches; but space is vast, and only in comparison is mankind's place in it tiny. Actually the distances were so great that commerce and intercourse between the outer Worlds was no more than desultory. We were banded into a loose alliance known as the Ten Thousand Worlds, and did our best to keep our contacts firm.

We were normally peaceful, and wanted peace with this alien world of Veldq—the first aliens we'd encountered—but you can't talk peace with a people who won't respond. Worse, they had obliterated the fleet bringing our initial peace overtures.

As a final gesture I had been smuggled in—in an attempt to breach that stand-off stubbornness. This booth at their Fair of Seasons was my best chance, as I saw it, to secure an audience with those in authority. And with luck it would serve a double purpose.

By now several Veldqans had read my sign, and gathered about my open-air booth, and watched with interest as my opponent and I chose colors. He took the red, I the black. We arranged our fifty-two pieces on their squares and I nodded to him to make the first move.

Have you ever played a game where the stake was your life? And perhaps even more? Nothing can compare with it. The slow flow of adrenalin into the bloodstream, bringing its fear-exultation stimulation, the doubts, the second thoughts, and yet with it all the conviction that you would change places with no man.

My opponent was an anemic oldster, with an air of nervous energy, and he played the same way, with intense concentration. By the fourth move I knew he would not win. On each play he had to consult the value board suspended between us before deciding on his next move. On a play board with one hundred and sixty-nine squares, each with a different value— in fact, one set of values for offense, and another for defense— only a brilliant player could keep them all in mind. But no man who couldn't was going to beat me.

I let him win the first game. Deliberately. The "second game counts" gimmick was not only to attract attention, but to give me a chance to test a player's strength—and to find his weakness.

At the start of the second game the oldster moved his front-row-center pukt three squares forward and one left oblique. I checked it with an end pukt and waited.

The contest was not going to be exacting enough to hold my complete attention. Already an intuitive portion of my mind—which I thought of as a small machine, ticking away in one corner of my skull, independent of any control or direction from me—was moving its interest out over the fair-grounds, and back to the spectators around my booth.

Every object about me, every passing face, would make its picture in the memory banks of that machine and wait there to be recalled. Further, it catalogued each fact learned or observed, in its proper relation to the others already there. Sometimes the addition of one new fact would cause it to give an almost audible click, and a conclusion, or an answer, seemingly unrelated to the final acquired fact, lay clear before me. The best simile I could think of was that of a penny scale, spitting out a card of fortune as a penny is dropped in. It constantly amazed me.

Most men, I presume, would regard a visual-recall memory as a very desirable asset. Some, a bit more introspective, would wonder if it might not be a curse. The latter would be more nearly correct. To me it was another mouth, a hungry mouth, that had to be fed constantly, or again, a load on my shoulders, that was being piled higher and higher, until one day I would slowly fold beneath the weight of it.

The other part of my mind idly carried on the action of the game and in three short moves I maneuvered a pukt four rows forward. From that particular square it could be moved a maximum of three paces forward, two left oblique, or three right oblique—with unlimited side and backward movement.

The old one moved to intercept my pukt, and I split his force apart with two men I had set in strategic positions on each side.

The roving portion of my mind caught a half-completed gesture of admiration at the sudden completion of the trap from a youth directly ahead of me. And with the motion, and the glimpse of the youth's face, something slipped into place in my memory. Some subconscious counting finished itself, and I knew that there had been too many of these youths, with faces like this one, finely honed and smooth, with slender delicate necks and slim hands and movements that were cool and detached. Far too many to be a normal number in a population of adults and children.

As though drawn, my glance went past the forms of the watchers around the booth and plumbed the passing crowd to the figure of a man, a magnificent masculine type of the Veldqan race, thick-shouldered and strong, careful in motion, yet with something of the swagger of a gladiator, who, as he walked, spoke to the woman who held his arm, leaning toward her cherishingly as if he protected a great prize.

She was wearing a concealing cloak, but her face was beautiful, her hair semi-long, and in spite of the cloak, I could see that her body was full-fleshed and almost voluptuously feminine. I had seen few such women on Veldq.

Two of the slim, delicately built youths went by arm in arm, walking with a slight defiant sway of bodies, and looked at the couple as they passed, with pleasure in the way the man's fascinated attention clove to the woman, and looked at the beauty of the woman possessively without lust, and passed by, their heads held higher in pride as though they shared a secret triumph with her. Yet they were strangers.

And I had an answer to my "counting." The "youths" with their large eyes and smooth, delicate heads, with the slim straight asexual bodies, thought of themselves as women. I had not seen them treated with the subdued attraction and conscious avoidance one sex gives another, but by the average.... My memory added the number of these "youths" to the number of figures and faces that had been obviously female. It totaled almost half the population I had seen. No matter what the biological explanation, it seemed reasonable that half....

I bent my head, to avoid seeing the enigma of the boy-woman face observing me, and braced my elbow to steady my hand as I moved. For two weeks I had been on Veldq and during the second week I had come out of hiding and passed as a Veldqan. It was incredible that I had been operating under a misunderstanding as to which were women and which were men, and not blundered openly. The luck that had saved me had been undeserved.

"There was so much to be learned, and so little time to do it in." I had a better appreciation then of the poet's meaning.

Opposite me, across the board, the bleached-skinned hand of the oldster was beginning to waver with indecision as each pukt was placed. He was seeing defeat, and not wishing to see it.

In four more minutes I completed the route of his forces and closed out the game. In winning I had lost only two pukts. The other's defeat was crushing, but my ruthlessness had been deliberate. I wanted my reputation to spread.

My sign, and the game in progress, by now had attracted a line of challengers, but as the oldster left, the line broke and most of the prospective challengers shook their heads and moved back, then crowded forward around the booth and good-naturedly elbowed their way to positions of better vantage.

I knew then that I had set my lure with an irresistible bait. On a world where the Game was played from earliest child-hood—was in fact a vital aspect of the culture—my challenge could not be ignored. I pocketed the loser's blue slip and nodded to the first in line of the four men still waiting to try me.

The second man played a better game than the old one. He had a fine tight-knit offense, with a good grasp of values, but his weakness showed early in the game when I saw him hesitate and waver before making a simple move in a defensive play. He was not skilled in the strategy of retreat and defense, or not suited to it by temperament. He would be unable to cope with a swift forward press, I decided.

I was right.

I played all through the long afternoon. Some challengers wagered more, some less, all lost on the second game. As Veldq's huge red sun slipped below the horizon I had a period when no one offered to contest me, and I purchased a nut and fruit confection from a passing food vendor for a sparse lunch.

The evening darkened as I rested, and soon floating particles of light-reflecting air foam began drifting over the Fair crowd. Somehow they were held suspended above the grounds while air currents tossed them about and intermingled them in the radiance of vari-hued spotlights. The grounds were still bright as day, but filled with long shifting shadows that seemed to heighten the byplay of sound and subdued excitement coming from the Fair visitors.

As I resumed the games I could tell by the gathering crowd about my booth that word of my presence had spread, but though the crowd was larger, the players were fewer. Sometimes I had a break of several minutes before one made a decision to try his skill. And there were no more challenges from ordinary players. Still the results were the same. None had sufficient adroitness to give me more than a passing contest.

Until Caertin Vlosmin made his appearance.

At the beginning of the game with Vlosmin I had no way of knowing that his game would be different. I noted only casually that he introduced himself rather formally before sitting, but I marked it as merely the exact manners of a conservative man, or a desire for ostentation. I was little interested in which.

I did realize from the first that he was a shrewd man, probably with a system. He lost the first game—without struggle. That, of course, was to keep me from learning anything about what he could do. I heeded the warning only enough to keep my attention more closely on the board as the second game began.

Vlosmin kept his pukts well back and closely grouped, making only a perfunctory display of aggressiveness. After a few minutes of innocuous interplay I tried him out by exposing a pukt at the edge of the board to my right. When he ignored it my estimation of his ability adjusted itself upward. He had readily recognized that a pukt, protected on one side by the playing edge, was not as vulnerable as it might seem to be.

I made several other feints—which he ignored. He would not come out to meet a pass, yet he tried no offensive forays of his own.

I presented three tentative exposures, all ignored, before I deliberately sent a pukt a bit too deep. I had made a pretense of setting up a defense for it in advance, but had left a small avenue of vulnerability. A man with an exceptionally good grasp of the positions on the board would have spotted it. Vlosmin studied the pieces for a long time, glancing twice at the value board, before he passed the pukt by.

I had found his weaknesses—both of them.

The man played a game intended to be impregnably defensive, which he would then use to advantage. But this mental prowess was not quite great enough to be certain of a sufficiently concealed or complex weakness in the approach of an adversary, and he would not hazard an attack on an uncertainty. Excess caution was his first weakness.

His second was exposed by his glances at the value board. They were not long enough for actual study. I'm certain that he did not even see what he glanced at: he had all the values well in mind. They were an expression of a small lack of confidence.

I should be able to exploit both.

Play by careful play I moved the entire body of my pukts forward, presenting him with the necessity of planning a completely new offense. The potency of the pukts being determined, not by an intrinsic value of their own, but by the position of the squares on which they rested, made the forward shift of the mass of my pukts a vast problem of realignment—for him. Each new pukt now had a new value, and Vlosmin had to adjust to that complete new set of factors.

During the play I sensed that the crowd about us was very intent and still. On the outskirts, newcomers inquiring cheerfully, were silenced by whispered injunctions.

The limit of Vlosmin's ability showed at my first pass in the new alignment. He became confused, hesitated too long before the pukt I exposed, and made a misplay in passing it up. I took the man he had used in passing. A minute later he lost another. He saw he was losing, and tried a total reversal of tactics, the desperate gamble of a V penetration at center.

Though it required all my concentration the game was soon over. I looked up as Vlosmin rose to his feet, and noted with surprise that a fine spray of perspiration dotted his upper lip. Only then did I recognize the strain and effort he had invested in the attempt to defeat me.

"You are an exceptional craftsman," Vlosmin said. There was a grave emphasis he put on the "exceptional" that I could not miss, and I saw that his face had lost some of its color. His formal introduction of himself earlier as "Caertin Vlosmin" had meant more than I realized at the time.

I had just played against, and defeated, one of Veldq's Great Players.

For the moment there were no more challengers. Around my booth all was quiet, the spectators subdued, as though waiting for the next act in a tense drama. I was very tired by now, but I knew by the stillness I observed all about me that I would not have much longer to wait.

I took advantage of the pause to stop a food and drink peddler again, and this time bought an almond-flavored liquid, and sipped at it while I looked about beneath lowered eyelids.

The peddler stayed a moment, his face displaying an expression that might have been amusement. His coffee-stain complexion proclaimed him a member of the Kisman clan, as were most all the tradesmen of Veldq. I had learned something about them earlier—they presented a fascinating study in their own right.

Their history, alone among the clans, had not been shaped by the eons-long struggle with the voracious dleeths. The animals apparently had a near-phobic fear of water, and had never invaded the Kismans' homeland, located on a large island in the South Rim Sea.

Because of that single but dominant factor, the Kismans' history and cultural mores were markedly different from those of the other clans. The Kismans were less inhibited, and lacked the unbending natures of the others; in comparison they might even be considered obsequious. However, they smiled more, and laughed more, and on the whole were happier, I judged.

They were tradesmen by nature and inclination, and with the coming of peace many had left their island and brought their mercantile skills to every available market. They were disdained by the other clansmen, as a lower class, and tolerated only because of their utility. Which humble state they accepted, seemingly without resentment.

The peddler here reminded me of Iten the shoemaker, with whom I had done business shortly after arriving on Veldq, searching for a comfortable pair of shoes. Most Veldqans wore boots, sturdy and long-lasting, but heavy, and to me cumbersome, adding to my difficulty in coping with Veldq's heavier gravity.

The bootmaker had made the shoes to my specifications while I waited, and I had taken the opportunity to acquire information with idle chatter—innocuous-sounding, I hoped—while he worked.

I was startled, and mildly amused, when he finished and presented his charges: nineteen dronkers for the shoes—a sum I had negotiated beforehand—and seven dronkers for information. "It is a commodity, you understand," Iten explained blandly. "I am certain you will find it of considerable value." He eyed me obliquely, waiting to smile or to argue, depending on my reaction. The man was a bit of a rogue, I guessed.

We laughed together then, both appreciating the humor of his temerity, and I paid without undue rancor.

The following morning I returned to Iten's place of business. "This day I wish to purchase information only," I informed him. "But you must convey it with conditions. You will play a child's game with me. We will pretend that I am an outlander, from a far province, with little knowledge of the City. My questions will seem to you very simple, perhaps even absurd, but you must humor me, and answer them with all seriousness. Do we have that agreement?"

"I will pretend that you have an impairment of the head." Iten acquiesced readily, and laughed, with undue merriment, I thought, until I reinterpreted the phrase more exactly. He had intimated that I could be insane. Which he might actually believe. It suited me fine.

"Who rules the City?" I began my series of questions.

When I finished my inquiries the pirate charged me an outrageous thirty dronkers. I groaned in semi-jest, but paid without further protest—confirming to him, I'm certain, his belief that I had an "impairment of the head." To me the information I received was priceless.

As I left him, Iten pontificated, "May there be only enough clouds in your day to furnish a beautiful sunset."

By the bubbles' light I watched as new spectators took their positions about my booth. And as time went by I saw that some did not move on, as my earlier visitors had done.

The weight that rode my stomach muscles grew abruptly heavier. I had set my net with all the audacity of a spider waiting for a fly, yet I knew that when my anticipated victim arrived he would more likely resemble a spider hawk. Still the weight in my stomach was not caused by fear. It was excitement—excitement about a larger game about to begin.

2

I was playing another opponent, stern faced and skillful, but with recognizably less ability than Vlosmin, when I heard a stirring and murmuring in the crowd around my stand. It was punctuated by my opponent rising to his feet.

I glanced up.

The big man who had walked into my booth was neither arrogant nor condescending, yet the confidence in his manner was like an aura of strength. He had a deep reserve of vitality, I noted as I studied him swiftly, but it was a leashed, controlled vitality. Like most men of the Veldqan race he wore a uniform, cut severely plain, and undecorated. No flowing robes or tunics for these men. They were a warrior race, unconcerned with the esthetic touches of personal dress, and left that strictly to their women.

The newcomer turned to my late opponent. "Please finish your game," he said courteously. His voice was impressive, controlled.

The stern faced man shook his head. "The game is already over. My sword has been broken. You are welcome to my place."

The tall man turned to me. "If you have no objections?" he asked.

"It is my pleasure," I answered carefully.

And the moment had arrived.

For a brief interval the air about me seemed to grow thin, inadequate for proper breathing, but I made an effort not to reveal my sudden discomfort. This was not the time to display weakness.

My visitor shrugged back his close-wrapped cloak and took the chair opposite me. "I am Kalin Trobt," he said, as though I had been expecting him.

I had been expecting someone in authority, but hadn't dared hope for anyone this high up. Kalin Trobt was Veldq's highest official.

In reply I very nearly gave Trobt my correct name. But Leonard Stromberg would have been strange to this world, and certain to reveal my identity as an alien. "Claustil Anteer," I said, giving a name I had invented earlier.

We played the first game as children play it, taking each other's pukts as the opportunity presented, making no attempt at finesse. Trobt won, two up. Neither of us made a mention of a wager, there would be more than money at stake in this Game.

I noticed, when I glanced up before the second Game began, that the spectators had been cleared from around the booth. Only the inner, unmoving ring I had observed earlier remained. They watched calmly. Professionally.

Fortunately I had no intention of trying to escape.

During the early part of the second Game Trobt and I tested carefully, like skilled swordsmen, probing, feinting, and shamming attack, but never actually exposing ourselves. I detected what could have been a slight tendency to gamble in Trobt's game, but there was no concrete confirmation.

After a short period of watchful stalking Trobt made a move I was totally unprepared for—a four-across-the-board exposed pukt. I could have taken it, of course, but to do so would have meant breaking formation and planning a new gambit. It took me several minutes to decide against the reply. The exposure was just too obvious. I countered cautiously, and he moved a second pukt, and a third up beside the first—space three squares apart. The pattern was forming—for my defeat.

The formation he had drawn up was almost unique—an intricate version of the diversified decoy gambit. I knew then that I would have to give my best to win. And that best might not be good enough!

I had learned the greater part of what I knew of the Game in the stalls of the marketplace. Most of the players there had been quite average, but better players made frequent visits in search of a contest, or to practice new strategies, and I had learned much from them. They had often discussed the various systems of play, and one of the most discussed had been the simple decoy gambits. These were intricate enough to take the normal player to the limits of his ability.

Double decoy gambits had been mentioned in passing, but had not been gone into deeply. They were just too complex for any but Masters, and even then required years of study—backed by great mental acuity.

They involved the use of abstract and negative reasoning that reminded me of the old Earth puzzler about the red and green circles painted on the foreheads of three wise men.

Yet Trobt was presenting a triple decoy gambit. The involvements of threat and counterthreat, action and counter action, the permutations of thrust and reply—and counter reply—were so numerous that it was impossible for me to conceive of a mind that could evaluate, control, and select the moves necessary to employ it properly. From my experience I was certain no Human on the Ten Thousand Worlds could effectively deploy such a gambit. Was it possible that these non-Humans could?

It would be foolhardy, I decided, to plunge ahead on an unverified assumption. I held back, grouping my side pukts into two wedges—facing left oblique—in what I had privately named my Rock-of-Gibralter defense. With this there was very little flexibility: a single pukt, operating at the mouth formed by the wedges, was my only mobile unit of offense. But as a defense it was very nearly impregnable—except perhaps to a triple decoy gambit.

Trobt made several further moves before he abruptly shifted the formation of his forces and assumed another pattern. I saw immediately then that what I had suspected earlier was true. His center decoy had been a blind. His actual play would be

made around the two outside points. The triple decoy attack
with which it seemed I had been threatened had been a trap
within a trap.

Only then did I allow myself to think of tactics and replies.
If I had responded to his first ruses, taking the triple decoy
formation seriously, I would by this time have been weltering
in half-begun, wasted formations of defense. It had taken self-
restraint to wait and make no reply to the first threat, but my
caution had been vindicated.

I flattened out my right peak and moved my side pukts up
to a position from which they could maneuver, or attack.

My first moves were entirely passive. Alertly passive. If I
had correctly judged the character of the big man opposite me,
I had only to ignore the bait he offered, to draw me out, to
disregard his openings, and apparent—too apparent—errors,
until he became convinced that I was unshakably cautious,
and not to be tempted into making the first thrusts. For this
was his weakness as I had assessed it: that his was a gambling
temperament—that when he saw an opportunity he would
strike—without the caution necessary to insure safety.

Pretending to move with timidity, and pausing with great
deliberation over even the most obvious plays, I maneuvered
only to defend. Each time Trobt shifted to a new position of
attack I covered—until finally I detected the use of slightly
more arm force than necessary when he moved a pukt. It was
the only sign of impatience he gave, but it was definitely there.
And it was what I had been waiting for.

Then it was that I left one—thin—opening.

Trobt streaked a pukt through and cut out one of my middle
defenders.

Instead of making the obvious counter of taking his piece
I played a pukt far removed from his invading man. He frowned
in concentration, and countered by taking a pukt I had exposed
in the move; we exchanged two more, and a third pair.

And Trobt's hand hung suspended above the board.

Suddenly his eyes widened, and his glance swept up to
mine. He had seen that he had the choice of exchanging two
more pukts or losing them without reply—after which his left
flank of twenty-two pukts would be cut off and helpless. He
read in my eyes that he had been maneuvered into a position

from which there was no safe retreat. His expression changed
to one of mingled astonishment and dismay.

He had lost the game.

Abruptly he leaned forward, touched his index finger to the
tip of my nose, and pressed gently.

After a minute during which neither of us spoke, I said,
"You know?"

He nodded. "Yes," he said. "You are a Human."

There was a stir and rustle of motion around me. The ring
of spectators had leaned forward a little as they heard his words.
I looked up and saw that they were smiling, inspecting me
with curiosity, and something that could have been called
admiration. In the shadows the clearest view was the ring of
teeth, gleaming—the view a rabbit might get of a circle of
grinning foxes. Foxes might feel friendly toward rabbits, and
admire a good big one. Why not?

I suppressed an ineffectual impulse to deny what I was. The
time for that was past. "How did you learn?" I asked Trobt.

"Your Game. No one could play like that and not be well-
known. And now your nose."

"My nose?" I repeated.

"Only one physical difference between a Human and a
Veldqan is apparent on the surface. The cartilage at the tips
of our noses. Yours is split; mine is single." He rose to his feet.
"Will you come with me, please?"

It was not a request.

My guards walked singly and in couples, sometimes passing
Trobt and myself, sometimes letting us pass them, and sometimes lingering at a booth like any other walkers, and yet they
held me encircled, unobtrusively, always in the center of the
group. I had already learned enough about the Veldqan per-
sonality to realize that this was simply a habit of tact. Tact to
prevent an arrest from being conspicuous, so as not to add the
gaze of his fellows to whatever punishment would be decided
on for a culprit's offense. Apparently they considered humiliation too grave a punishment to be used indiscriminately.

At first thought it seemed incongruous that a race I had
found to be excessively proud, warlike, merciless in conflict,

and often downright irascible should be so courteous. However, the answer was obvious with a bit more consideration. On Veldq, unless one deliberately sought lethal contention he was wise to make certain his manners were impeccable. And this consideration for others had by now become a part of their natures.

We had had similar periods of high courtesy in our Earth history. Gallantry and courteous behavior were never greater than when dueling had been the fashion in ancient France and England.

The Veldqans had an almost dogmatic insistence on the rigid observance of social rites and custom. And there lay perhaps my greatest danger. My eidetic memory could be of exceptional aid to me in learning another race's language, and in many other ways here, but unless a person lives in and with a culture for many years, he can never understand all its nuances and inflections. A dozen times a day in the past two weeks I had used words or expressions that caused my listeners to raise their eyebrows. Probably the only reason I had gotten by was that they had not been expecting to find someone such as myself among them—and marked my speech as mere idiosyncrasy.

At the edge of the Fairgrounds some of my guards bunched around me while others went to get their tricars. I stood and looked across the park to The City. That was what it was called. The City, The Citadel, The Homeplace, where one's family is kept safe, the sanctuary whose walls have never been breached. All those connotations had been in the name and the use of the name, and in the voices of those who spoke it. Sometimes they called it The Hearth, and sometimes The Market, always *The,* as though it were the only one. Yet the speakers lived in other places and named them as the homes of their ancestors.

It was a puzzle.

I could see the Games Building from where I stood. In the walled city called Hearth it was the highest point. Big and red, it towered above the others, and the city around it rose to it like a wave, its consort of surrounding smaller buildings matched to each other in size and shape in concentric rings.

Around each building wound the ramps of elevator runways, harmonious and elegant, each of different colored stone, blending beautifully with the background and surroundings, lending variety and warmth. Nowhere was there a clash of either proportion or color. Sometimes I wondered if the Veldqans did not build more for the joy of symmetry than for utility.

I climbed into Trobt's three-wheeled car as it stopped in front of me, and the minute I settled back into the bucket seat and gripped the bracing handles, Trobt spun the car and it dived into the highway and rushed toward the City. The vehicle seemed unstable, being about the width of a motor bike with the sidecar in front, and having nothing behind except a metal box that must have housed a powerful battery, and a shaft connected with the rear wheel and used for steering. It was an arrangement that made possible sudden wrenching turns that battered any passenger as unused to it as I. To my conditioning it seemed that the Veldqans on the highway drove like madmen, the traffic rules incomprehensible or nonexistent, and all drivers determined to drive only in gull-like sweeping lines, giving no obvious change of course for other such cars, brushing by tricars coming from the opposite direction with an inch or less of clearance.

Apparently the maneuverability of the cars and the skill of the drivers were enough to prevent accidents, and I had to force my totally illogical driver's reflexes to relax and stop tensing against the nonexistent peril.

I watched Trobts' hands moving on the controls, empathizing with him as he drove, letting the technique and coordination of steering the three-wheeled vehicle imprint itself on my memory, where I might soon find a use for it.

Also, I studied Trobt himself, noting the casual way he held the wheel, and the assurance in the set of his shoulders. I tried to imagine what kind of man he was, and just what the motivations were that would move or drive him. Knowing that would be more important than learning to handle the tricar.

Physically he was a long-faced man, with a smooth muscular symmetry, and an Asiatic cast to his eyes. I was certain that he excelled at whatever job he held. In fact I was prepared to

believe that he would excel at anything he tried. He was undoubtedly one of those amazing men for whom the exceptional
was mere routine. If he were to be cast in the role of my
opponent, be the person in whom the opposition of this race
was to be actualized—as I now anticipated—I would not have
wanted to bet against him.

The big skilled man was silent for several minutes, weaving
the tricar with smooth swerves through a three-way tangle at
an intersection, but twice he glanced at my expression with
evident curiosity. Finally, as a man would state an obvious
fact, he said, "I presume you know you will be executed?"

Trobt's face reflected surprise at the shock he must have
read in mine. I had known the risk I would be taking in coming
here, of course, and of the very real danger of my ultimate
death. But this had come up on me too fast. I had not realized
that the affair had progressed to the point where my death was
already assured. I had thought that there would be negotiations,
consultations, and perhaps ultimatums. But only if they failed
did I believe that the repercussions might carry me along to
my death.

However, there was the possibility, I reasoned quickly, that
Trobt was merely testing my courage, perhaps even toying with
me to watch my reactions. During the last few days I had
prepared several arguments to use when needed—the time
might never be more appropriate.

"No," I said. "I do not expect to be executed."

Trobt's expression became perplexed, and he slowed, pre-
sumably to gain more time to talk. With sudden decision he
swung the tricar from the road into one of the small parks
spread at regular intervals along the roadway.

"Surely you did not think that we would permit you to live?
There's a state of war between Veldq and your Ten Thousand
Worlds. You admit you're Human, and obviously you are here
to spy. Yet when you are captured, you do not expect to be
executed?"

"Was I captured?" I asked, emphasizing the last word.

He pondered on that for a minute, but apparently did not
come up with an answer that satisfied him. "I am afraid the
subtlety of that question escapes me," he said at the end.

"If I had wanted to keep my presence here a secret, would I have set up a booth at the Fair and invited inspection?" I asked.

Trobt waved one hand irritably, as though to brush aside a picayune argument. "Obviously you did it to test yourself against us, to draw the Great under your eye, and perhaps become a friend, treated as an equal, with access to knowledge of our plans and weapons. Certainly! Your tactics drew two members of the Council into your net before it was understood. If we had accepted you as a previously unknown Great, you would have won. You are a gambling man, and you played a gambler's hand. You lost."

"Give that another moment of thought," I countered, a bit angry myself at what might have been meant as an insult. "I'm not a fool. I've been on your world a total of fourteen days. How much do you think I know of it, and of your society? What do I know of your customs, your history, your geography, or a hundred other aspects of how you live and act? Wouldn't I understand how quickly you'd discover the deception if I tried to pass myself as one of you? Surely I would never have attempted it without better preparation."

Partly what Trobt had said had been correct. I had hoped to win acceptance of a kind, by exhibiting my proficiency in the Game. With all its ramifications in the Veldqan culture that would have been important: in a warrior society individual achievement weighs heavily. If I could prove to them that I was worthy of the task I had undertaken they might give me a receptive audience—while it could be withheld from one who had not proven himself. As I saw it.

Trobt did not reply, remaining silent and motionless for several long minutes, lost in a self-imposed isolation. I noted his abstraction, and wondered if it might not be wise to seize control of the tricar and attempt to escape. I made a rapid survey of our immediate surroundings, the road, the fields to our right, and the City in the near distance. I studied also the soldiers around us, noting how they chatted idly, with little of their attention on Trobt and me.

I decided quickly against the impulse, however. It was thoroughly illogical, promoted by a mild form of panic. Trobt was big, and catlike in motion, and not handicapped by an unaccustomed weight of gravity as I was. His men would respond swiftly, I knew, despite their apparent laxness now. And if by some fortunate chance I were able to escape, how long would I be able to remain free?

Yet even as I rejected the temptation to be foolhardy, I wondered in passing if there might be a criminal element in the City, among whom I could lose myself.

My attention switched back to Trobt. He was still immersed in thought, very probably giving grave consideration to what had transpired between us thus far. Perhaps I could influence his final decision with a proper interjection, I hazarded. "My only intention in setting up my booth was to reach you, or someone else with sufficient authority to listen to what I have to say," I tried.

Trobt nodded, my words apparently concurring with some conclusion he had already formed. He did not answer, however, instead taking the wheel of his vehicle and driving deeper into the park. Afterward he waited while the cars of our escort settled into place ahead of and behind us. Only then did he break his silence.

"Speak then," he said. "I will listen." I thought I detected a measure of restraint and rigidity in his manner.

"My purpose in coming here was to negotiate," I told him. "I hope to reach a peaceful solution to our difficulties."

"You are serious," he stated, when I paused, seemingly incredulous at what I had proposed.

"Very much so. If we could arrive at an agreement it would save countless lives, and avert the massive destructions of a war. Could anyone object to that?"

Something like a flash of puzzlement crossed his features before they returned to tighter immobility. Unexpectedly he spoke in Earthian, my own language! "Why then did you choose this method? Would it not have been better simply to announce yourself?"

Earthian. The implications rushed through me and plucked at my nerves. Originally we Humans had supposed that there had been no contact between Veldq and the Ten Thousand Worlds Federation. I had had my own suspicions, however, and promoted my own investigation. I had learned that at least one Veldqan had visited our Worlds—but had not expected to find him this readily. The discovery left me with the necessity of realigning my strategy somewhat. Also, my anticipated arguments had to undergo some alteration.

Doing my best to hide my reaction to his change of language, I replied, still speaking Veldqan, "Would it have been that simple? Or would some minor official, on capturing me, perhaps have had me imprisoned or tortured to extract information?"

Trobt pondered the back of one hand, before returning his gaze to me. "They would have treated you as an envoy of your Ten Thousand Worlds. You could have spoken to the Council immediately." He spoke Veldqan now. "It would have changed nothing, however. You are bringing an insult, whether from your Worlds or from yourself, and the Council would never have accepted your overtures." He added, "And in the end you would still have had to die."

"Then there has been very little lost," I said fatalistically, and felt myself growing angry again. "Talking to you is apparently an exercise in futility," I declared. "You and your race are so stubborn that reason is wasted on you."

The brief play of emotion in Trobt's face was not quite anger, and not quite resentment. I wanted desperately to interpret it, for if I knew what emotion it was reflecting I could make better use of any future arguments. Despite my words to him I still had hopes of reaching some reasonable settlement here. I failed to read his reaction, however; I knew only that it was nothing shallow.

Trobt began to speak, but his voice came out higher than he had intended, I saw, embarrassing him slightly, and he forced himself to be more placid as he turned in his seat to face me directly. His gaze was level and steady, his expression unreadable. "Tell me what you have to say then," he directed, obviously making a considerable concession. "I will judge whether or not the Council should hear you."

"To begin . . ." I looked away from the expressionless eyes, out the windshield, down the vista of short brown trees that grew between each small park and the next. "Until an exploring party of ours found signs of extensive mining operations on a small metal-rich planet, we knew nothing of your existence.

We were not even aware that another intelligent race existed in the galaxy, and that it had discovered faster-than-light travel. But after that first clue we were alert to other signs, and found them. Our discovery of your planet was bound to come. However, we did not expect to be met on our first visit with an attack of such hostility as you displayed."

"When we learned that you had found us," Trobt said, without heat, "we sent a message to your Ten Thousand Worlds, warning that we wanted no contact. Yet you sent a fleet of spaceships against us."

I hesitated before answering, "That phrase 'sent against us,' is hardly the correct one," I said. "The fleet was sent for a diplomatic visit, and was not meant as an aggressive action." I thought, *But obviously the display of force was intended "diplomatically" to frighten you people into being polite. In diplomacy the smile, the extended hand—and the big stick visible in the other hand—have averted many a war, by giving the stranger a chance to choose a hand, in full understanding of the alternative. We showed our muscle to your little planet— you showed your muscle. And now we are ready to be polite.*

I had hoped these people would understand the face-saving ritual of negotiation, the disclaimers of intent, that would enable each side to claim that there had been no fight, merely accident. "We did not at all feel that you were justified in wiping our fleet from space," I said, "but it was probably a legitimate misunderstanding—"

"You had been warned!" Trobt's voice was grim, his expression not inviting further discussion. I thought I detected a bunching of the muscles in his jawline.

For a moment I said nothing, made no gesture, letting the subject go by. Apparently this angle of approach was non-productive—and probably explosive. Also, trying to explain and justify the behavior of the Federation politicos could possibly become rather taxing.

"Surely you don't intend to postpone negotiations indefinitely?" I asked tentatively. "One planet cannot conquer the entire Federation."

Trobt's back straightened, making him appear taller than before, and his lips thinned with the effort of controlling some savage anger. Apparently my question had affronted his pride.

This, I decided quickly, was not the time to make an enemy. "I apologize if I have insulted you," I said in Earthian. "I do not always understand what I am saying, in your language."

He hesitated, made some kind of effort, and shifted to Earthian. "It is not a matter of strength or weakness," he said, letting his words ride out on his released breath, "but on behavior, courtesy. We would have left you alone, but now it is too late. We will drive your faces into the ground. I am certain that we can, but if we could not, still we would try. To imply that we would not try, from fear, seems to me words to soil the mouth, not worthy of a man speaking to a man. We are converting our ships of commerce to war ships. Your people will see soon that we will fight."

"Is it too late for negotiations?" I tried once again.

His forehead wrinkled in a frown and he stared at me in an effort of concentration. When he spoke it was with a considered hesitation. "If I make an effort, a great effort, I can feel that you are sincere, and not speaking to mock or insult. It is strange that beings who look so much like ourselves can . . ." He passed a hand across his eyes. "Pause a moment. When I say *yag loogt' n 'balt* what does it mean to you in Earthian?"

"I must play." I hesitated as he turned one hand palm down, signifying that I was wrong. "I must duel?" I said, finding another meaning in the way I had heard the phrase expressed. It was a strong meaning, judging by the tone and inflection the speaker used. I had mimicked the tone without full understanding. The verb was perhaps stronger than *must*, meaning something inescapable, fated, but I could find no Earthian verb for it. I understood why Trobt dropped his hand to the seat without turning it palm up to signify that I was correct.

"There must be no such thought on the Human worlds," he said resignedly. "I have to explain as to a child or a madman. I cannot explain in Veldqan, it has no word to explain what needs no explanation."

He shifted to Earthian, his controlled voice sounding less firm when moving with the more fluid inflections of my own tongue. "We said we did not want further contact. Nevertheless you sent the ships—deliberately in disregard of our expressed desire. That was an insult, a deep insult, meaning we have not the strength to defend our word, meaning we are so helpless that we can be treated with impoliteness, like prisoners, or infants.

"Now we must show you which of us is helpless, which is the weakling. Since you would not respect our wishes, then in order not to be further insulted we must make of your people a captive or a child in helplessness, so that you will be without power to affront us another time."

"If apologies are in order—"

He interrupted with a raised hand, still regarding me very earnestly, with forehead wrinkled, thought half turned inward in difficult introspection of his own meaning, as well as grasping for my viewpoint.

"The insult of the fleet can be wiped out only in the blood of testing—of battle—and the test will not stop until one or the other shows that he is too weak to struggle, lying without defense. There is no other way."

He was demanding total surrender!

I saw that it was a subject which could not be debated. The Federation had taken on a bearcat this time!

3

Night was well along now and very dim yellow lights shone in some windows of the larger buildings in the City, but there were no lights except those of our cars along the shadowy street where we had parked our convoy.

Kalin Trobt, military strategist, member of the Advisory Council of Veldq—I had learned from Iten the shoemaker—gazed along the street in the direction we were to go. "I stopped because I wanted to understand you," he said, "because others will not understand how you could be an envoy—how your Federation could send an envoy—except as an insult. I have seen enough of Human strangeness not to be maddened by the insolence of an emissary coming to us, or by your people expecting us to exchange words when we carry your first insult still unwashed from our faces. I can see even how it could perhaps be considered *not* an insult, for I have seen your people living on their planets and they suffered insult from each other without striking, until finally I saw that they did not know when they were insulted, as a deaf man does not know when his name is called."

I observed the quiet tone of his voice, trying to recognize the attitude that made it different from his previous tones—

29

calm, slow and deep—certainty that what he was saying was important—conscious tolerance—generosity.

He turned on the tricar's motor and put his hands on the steering shaft. "You are a man worthy of respect," he said, looking down the dark empty road ahead. "I wanted you to understand us. To see the difference between us. So that you will not think us without justice." The car began to move. "I wanted you to understand why it is inevitable that you will die."

I said nothing, having nothing to say. But I began immediately to bring my report up to date, recording the observations during the games, and recording with care this last conversation, with the explanation it carried of the Veldqan reactions, that had previously been obscure.

I used nerve-twitch code, "typing" on a tape somewhere inside myself the coded record of everything that had passed since the last time I brought the report up to date. This was valuable information.

The typing was simple, like flexing a finger in code jerks, but I did not know exactly where the recorder was located. It was some form of transparent plastic that would not show up on X ray. The surgeons had imbedded it in my flesh while I was unconscious, and had implanted a mental block against my noticing which small muscle had been linked into the contrivance for typing.

It would be worth a hazard to learn something about the Veldqan war equipment, and try to find a power source to broadcast the report back, but I did not see any immediate chance of access to that power source.

If I should die before I wake. . . .

If I died before I was able to return to Earth, I had been informed there were several capsuled chemicals buried at various places in my body, that intermingled would temporarily convert my body to a battery for a high-powered broadcast of the tape report, destroying the tape and my body together. This would go into action only if my temperature fell fifteen degrees below the temperature of life.

The thought of the chemicals was disturbing. I had informed my friend Lester Harvieux that I wanted to look in on Veldq, to see if our mutual problem could be solved by logic, and informed him that by....

I became aware that Kalin Trobt was speaking again, and that I had let my attention wander while recording, and taped some subjective material. The code twitches easily became an unconscious accompaniment to memory and thought, and this was the second time I had found myself recording more than was necessary.

We had reached the City by this time. Trobt kept his gaze on the dark thoroughfare, threading among buildings and past resting vehicles. His voice as he spoke was thoughtful. "In the early days, Miklas of Danlee, when he had the Ornan family surrounded and outnumbered, wished not to destroy them, for he needed good warriors, and in another circumstance they could have been friends. Therefore he sent a slave to them with an offer of terms of peace. The Ornan family had the slave skinned while alive, smeared with salt and grease so that he would not bleed, and sent back, tied in a bag of his own skin, with a message of no. The chroniclers agree that since the Ornan family was known to be honorable, Miklas should not have made the offer.

"In another time and battle, the Cheldos were offered terms of surrender by an envoy. Nevertheless they won against superior forces, and gave their captives to eat of a stew whose meat was the envoy of the offer to surrender. Made to eat their own words, as you'd say in Earthian. Such things are not done often, because the offer is not given."

He wrenched the steering post sideways and the tricar turned almost at right angles, balanced on one wheel for a dizzy moment, and fled up a great spiral ramp winding around the outside of the red Games Building.

Trobt looked ahead, steering the vehicle, but speaking to me. "I observe that you Earthians will lie without soiling the mouth. What are you here for, actually?"

"I came from interest, but I intend, given the opportunity, to observe and to report my observations back to my government. They should not enter a war without knowing anything about you."

"Good." For the first time he approved of a reply of mine.

He wrenched the car around another abrupt turn into a red archway in the side of the building, bringing it to a stop inside. The sound of the other tricars entering the tunnel echoed hollowly from the walls and died as they came to a stop around us. "You are a spy then?" Trobt said, as he climbed from the tricar.

"Yes," I said, getting out. I had silently resigned my commission as an envoy some five minutes earlier. There was little point in delivering political messages, if they had no result except to have one skinned alive or made into a stew.

A heavy door with the seal of an important official engraved upon it opened before us, and we walked into a large office-type room, permeated with a faint aroma of leather and dusty files. In the forepart of the room a slim-bodied creature with the face of a girl sat with crossed legs on a platform resembling a coffee table, sorting vellum marked with dots and dashes, arrows and pictures, of the Veldqan language. This was one of the boy-girls that had puzzled me. If I were to have the opportunity to get farther here I would have to learn more about them soon.

This one had green eyes, honeyed-olive complexion, a red mouth and purple-black hair. She finished figuring on an abacus-like instrument, made a notation on one of the stiff sheets of vellum, then glanced up to see who had entered. She observed us a moment, and glanced away again, as though she had made a note in her mind of our presence, and went back to her work stacking her vellum sheets on thin shelves with quick graceful motions.

"Kalin Trobt of Pagal," a man on the far side of the room called, a man sitting cross-legged on a dais covered with brown fur and scattered papers. He rose and came over to us and accepted the hands Trobt offered, each gripping the other by the wrists in locked gestures of friendship. "And how survive the other sons of the citadel of Pagal?" he greeted.

"Well, and continuing in friendship to the house of Lyagin," Trobt replied courteously. "I have seen little of my kin. There are many farlanders all around us, and between myself and my heartfolk swarm the adopted."

"It is not like in the old days, Kalin Trobt. In a dream I saw a rock sink with the weight of sons, and I longed for the sight of a land that is without strangers."

"We are all kinfolk now, Lyagin."

"My hearth pledged it."

We walked without attention back to Lyagin's dais, where he put a hand on a stack of missives he had been previously considering, his face thoughtful, sparsely fleshed, mostly skull and tendon, his hair bound back from his face, and wearing a short trouser garment beneath a light fur cape. A communicator stylus and a vision screen of some sort rested on a half-circle table surrounding his dais, and a short sword and long glaive formed a cross on the wall behind him. The weapons were made of bronze, or some bronze-colored metal.

I felt the annotator in my mind jump as it noted the bronze weapons. However, it was followed quickly by a "disregard" signal. The alert had come because the bronze weapons might have a story to tell concerning the historical stage of this civilization, and help me know it better and quicker. The disregard came with the recall that they had space travel. No race with that accomplishment would still be in its bronze age. I waited a minute and when nothing more came shifted my attention back to the vision screen.

I had seen them before, but I had not yet had an opportunity to study one closely. I would have liked to open it and learn if the same engineering techniques were involved as those of our vision masters. This set, as the others, was remarkably compact, being almost a flat screen, with a depth of only an inch or two behind the screen, and no attachments other than hand grips on the sides. All those I had seen were of the same size, their use universal, almost entirely for practical purposes, seldom for entertainment.

Lyagin was clearing his throat with a rasping sound and my attention returned to him. He was an old man, already senile, and now he stood lost in a lapse of awareness of what he had been doing a moment before. By no sign did Trobt show impatience, or even consciousness of the other's lapse.

Lyagin raised his head then and focused his rheumy eyes on us. "You brought someone in regard to an inquiry?" he asked Trobt.

"The one from the Ten Thousand Worlds." Trobt indicated me with an inclination of his head.

Lyagin nodded apologetically. "I received word that he would be brought," he said. He inspected me, going over my physique and stance with only meager interest. "He seems to be outwardly like a man, this outworlder. We will soon see if he be actually a man. How did you capture him?"

"He came."

The expression must have had some connotation that I did not recognize for the official let his glance rest on mine, and I caught one slight flicker of recognition to acknowledge that I was a person.

At that moment the boy-girl, still in my line of vision, glanced up from her work, directly at my face, my expression, then locked eyes with mine for a brief moment. The iris of her eyes shaded to a darker green, then quickly lightened again. When she glanced down to the vellum it was as though she had seen whatever she had looked up to see, and was content. She sat a little straighter as she worked, and moved with an action that was a little less supple and compliant.

I believe she had seen me as a man.

"He has the bearing of a hunter," Lyagin's voice interrupted my wandering thoughts. "Perhaps he may even prove to be a Man. (His tone capitalized the word.) If you want him questioned, we shall soon learn."

Quite apparently his words were meant as a compliment—conditionally. Their opinion of Humans was obviously not high. However, his words had had other intimations that were not pleasant. Again I thought: *This is moving too fast. My time is running out.*

"All I have seen of him indicates that he is an honorable enemy," Trobt said. "Until he proves otherwise I would suggest that he be treated as such a man."

I am a quite serious student of voice intonations and inflections and I was astonished to read sympathy in Trobt's tone.

Lyagin regarded him with obvious disapproval, and I realized that Trobt had gone beyond normal official disinterest in speaking for me. I wondered what had caused that intercession.

"I have heard that these Humans lie," Lyagin rebuked Trobt. "Is that honorable?"

"That is true." Trobt seemed to be trying to atone for his deviation from proper conduct. "They lie frequently. It is considered almost honorable to lie to an enemy in circumstances where one may profit by it. However," Trobt vacillated again, "this does not seem such a one. And he has already demonstrated his strength." He paused, and emphasized his next words. "He bested me in the Game."

"He bested you?" Lyagin's face showed all the astonishment his ancient features were capable of—before he came over and gripped both my wrists. I was beginning to feel somewhat hopeful, until he turned back to Trobt, and asked, "I believe you brought back from his worlds a poison that insures his speaking the truth before he dies?"

There again was that duality of Veldqan nature—Lyagin apparently had just congratulated me respectfully, yet that diverted him not at all from his—and Trobt's—intention to kill me.

"It is not a poison," Trobt replied, "but a chemical that affects one like strong drink, dulling his senses, and changing what he might do. Under its influence he loses his initiative of decision."

Trobt apparently had brought the truth drug from the Worlds in anticipation of taking Human prisoners, I decided. He was a farsighted man.

"You have this chemical with you?" Lyagin asked.

"I left it with Vay of the Hunt department," Trobt answered.

Despite my mental discomfort I marked yet another point of admiration for him. He was going to waste no time making use of me. I had much he wanted to learn, and he intended to get from me anything and everything that might be of value to his side.

Trobt was making no allowance for my state of near exhaustion. Rather, he was probably deliberately exploiting it, having his way with me when I had little strength to fight him. The quality of mercy . . . Most warrior cultures regard mercy as a weakness. Inwardly I resolved that getting the information from me would not be as easy as they might suppose.

Lyagin gripped one of the side handles on the vision screen

and squeezed, at the same time looking me over thoughtfully. "I had such information," he said to Trobt. "I'd allowed myself to forget it. I see now what its use will be. I have always distrusted torture for breaking a silence, and with such as he, there would be no surety that he spoke the truth—even with the torture. It will be interesting having an enemy cooperate. If he finds no way to kill himself, he can be very useful to us." Thus far my contact with the Veldqans had not been going at all as I had planned.

I was not whipped yet, however. They would learn that when the time came.

Lyagin held a note against the screen, which had begun flashing red. "It is ready," he said.

They injected the truth serum into my left hip.

I had little fear—even when I found that I was unable to tell a direct untruth under the drug's influence.

I answered each question they gave me. Questions that were intended to use my knowledge of the Ten Thousand Worlds against my race.

Most of the early night they probed for answers to our military strength, numbers of ships of war, potency of our weapons, and devices of strategy and tactics.

I made no attempt to resist the drug. I answered truthfully— but literally. Many times my answers were undecipherable— I did not know the answers, or lacked the data to give them. The others were cloaked under a full literal subtlety that made them useless to the Veldqans. Questions such as the degree of unity existing between the Worlds. I answered—truthfully— that they were united under an authority with supreme power of decision. The fact that that authority had no actual force behind it, that it was subject to the whims and fluctuations of sentiment and politics of inter-alliances, that it had deteriorated into a mere supernumerary body of impractical theorists, that occupied itself, in a practical sphere, only with picayune matters, I did not explain. It was not asked of me.

Would our Worlds fight? I answered that they would fight to the death to defend their liberty and independence. I did not add that that will to fight would evidence itself first in internal bickering, procrastinations, and jockeying to avoid the

worst thrusts of the enemy—before it finally resolved itself into
a united front against attack.

Trobt took no part in the early questioning. It was conducted
by Veldqans trained in that work. However, I could sense his
mounting dissatisfaction. He realized what was happening, but
he realized also that only someone with a background of culture
the same as mine would know how to phrase the questions so
as to get the answers he wanted—and to grasp the full meaning
of the answers when he got them.

By early morning Trobt could no longer contain his impatience. For the past hour he had been watching with his legs
spread and his face expressionless. However, his hands showed
his mounting frustration—toward the end they were either
closed in tight fists or spread wide open. Finally he walked to
where I sat.

"We are going to learn one thing," he said, his voice harsh.
"Why did you come here?"

"To learn all I could about you," I answered.

"You came to find a way to whip us!"

It was not a question and I had no need to answer.

"Have you found that way?" he asked.

"No."

"If you do, and you are able, will you use that knowledge
to kill us?" he pressed.

"No."

Trobt's eyebrows raised. "No?" he repeated. "Then why do
you want it?"

"I hope to find a solution that will not harm either side."

Trobt was puzzled with that answer. It verified what I had
been insisting from the first, but he had not believed me,
entirely. It was as though he had no conception of an enemy
seeking anything other than conquest. That was a small victory
for my side. "If you find that a solution is not possible," Trobt
resumed, "will you use that knowledge to defeat us?"

"Yes." Here I would have preferred not to answer.

"Even if it meant that you had to exterminate us—man and
child?"

It was my turn to be puzzled. I had not thought philo-
sophical considerations such as this were of much concern to
these warriors. My guess was that the question was prompted

more by Trobt's inquiring mind than by a characteristic racial curiosity. "Yes," I answered.

"Why? Are you so certain that you are right, that you walk with God, and that we are knaves?"

"I would have two considerations there. We are seeking peace, you are not. And, if the necessity to destroy one civilization or the other were mine to make, I would rule against you because of the number of sentient beings involved."

"What if the situation were reversed, and your side was in the minority? Would you choose to let them die?"

I bowed my head as I gave him the truthful answer. "I would choose for my own side, whatever the circumstances."

"I knew so."

And abruptly the interrogation was over.

On the drive to his home Trobt was once again the courteous, considerate captor. There was no trace in his tone or manner of the harshness that had been evident during the interrogation. He talked easily, and asked questions, but they were—apparently, at least—prompted only by friendly interest.

"How did you learn to play the Game so well?" he asked.

"I'm a player of the Human game called chess. Considered an adept. Much the same type of reasoning and tactics are involved in the two."

"That much I know," Trobt said. "You explained it while under the influence of the chemical."

For the first time then I realized that I did not have complete recall of everything I had said at the questioning. I had a moment of acute unease. It did not last, however. Whatever I had said, I was certain that my resolve to give them nothing of value had held firm throughout. And Trobt's manner and comments now indicated as much.

Not that his was an attitude of defeat. Rather it indicated that there was more to come.

By this time I was dead tired, and barely able to keep my eyes open. I would not be able to stay awake much longer. I realized with a start of surprise that Trobt was still talking. "... that a man with ability enough to be a Games—chess— master of nine planets is given no authority over his people, but merely consulted on occasional abstract questions of tactics."

"It is the nature of the problem." I had caught the gist of his comment from his last words and did my best to answer it. I wanted nothing less than to engage in conversation, but I realized that the interest he was showing now was just the kind I had tried to guide him to earlier in the evening. If I could get him to understand us better, our motivations and ideals, perhaps even our frailties, there would be more hope of a compatible meeting of minds. "Among people of such mixed natures, such diverse histories and philosophies, and different ways of life, most administrative problems are problems of a choice of whims, of changing and conflicting goals; not *how* to do what a people want done, but *what* they want done, and whether their next generation will want it enough to make work on it, now, worthwhile."

"They sound insane," Trobt said. "Are your administrators supposed to serve the flickering goals of demented minds?"

"We must weigh values. What is considered good may be a matter of viewpoint, and may change from place to place, from generation to generation. In determining how people feel and what their unvoiced wants are, a talent for strategy, and an impatience with the illogic of others, are not qualifications."

"The good is good, how can it change?" Trobt asked. "I do not understand."

I saw that truly he could not understand, since he had seen nothing of the clash of philosophies among a mixed people. He was having the same trouble understanding us as I was understanding them. Never the twain...

I tried to think of ways it could all be explained, how to show him that a people who let their emotions control them more than their logic, would unavoidably do many things they could not justify or take pride in—but that that emotional predominance was what had enabled them to grow, and spread throughout their section of the galaxy—and be, in the main, happy.

I was tired, achingly tired. More, the events of the long day, and Veldq's heavier gravity had taken me to the last stages of exhaustion. Yet I wanted to keep that weakness from Trobt.

It was quite possible that he, and the other Veldqans, would judge Humans by what they observed in me.

Trobt's attention was on his driving and he did not notice that I followed his conversation only with difficulty. "Have you had only the two weeks of practice in the Game since you came?" he asked.

I kept my eyes open with an effort, and breathed deeply. Veldq's one continent, capping the planet on its upper third, merely touched what would have been a temperate zone. During its short summer, which it was experiencing now, its mean temperature hung in the low sixties. At night it dropped to near freezing. The cold night air bit into my lungs and drove some of the fog of exhaustion from my brain.

"No," I answered Trobt's question, "I learned it before I came. A chess adept wrote me, in answer to an article on chess, that a man from one of the outworlds had beaten him in three games of chess after only two games to learn it, and had shown him a game of greater richness and flexibility than chess, with much the same feeling to the player, and had said that on his own planet this chess-like game was the basis for the amount of authority with which a man is invested. The stranger would not name his planet.

"I hired an investigating agency to learn the whereabouts of the planet. There was none in the Ten Thousand Worlds. That meant that the man had been a very ingenious liar, or—that he had come from Veldq."

"It was I, of course," Trobt acknowledged.

"I realized that from our conversation. The sender of the letter," I expanded, "was known to be a chess champion of two Worlds. The matter tantalized my thoughts for weeks, and finally I decided to visit Veldq. If you had this game, I wanted to try myself against your skilled ones."

"I understand that desire very well," Trobt said. "The same temptation caused me to be indiscreet when I visited your Worlds. I have seldom been able to resist the opportunity for an intellectual gambit." He smiled, for the first time, a surprisingly sunny smile.

"Even if you came intending to challenge," Trobt resumed, "you had little enough time to learn to play as you have—

against men who have spent lifetimes learning. I'd like to try you again soon, if I may."

"Certainly." I was in little mood or condition to welcome any further polite conversation. And I did not appreciate the irony of his request—to the best of my knowledge I was still under a sentence of early death.

Trobt must have caught the bleakness in my reply for he glanced quickly over his shoulder at me. "There is a saying, 'Each hour is a wound, the last one fatal.'" He saw readily that it was small consolation to me, and added, "There will be time. Several days at least. You will be my guest." I knew he was doing his best to be kind. His decision that I must die was not prompted by any meanness of nature. To him it was only—inevitable.

I could tell that Trobt had more to say, but he paused, as though fighting a natural inhibition. "You and I are much alike in our natures," he said, carefully selecting each word. "In different circumstances I am certain we would have been friends. I wish that we could be friends now."

I was too exhausted to return the compliment—though I had had the same feeling quite some time before.

We turned into a side street, and came to rest in front of a large teal-green building. Only then did I notice that we no longer had our escort. It was a weakness of mine that I often became lost in contemplation of some interesting subject, and missed much of the ordinary events and details going on about me. That faculty was an asset when matters arose requiring deep consideration, and I believe it was the principal factor in making me proficient in games such as chess—and the Game here. Its fault was that it led to small embarrassments—and friendly jokes at my expense, of the absent-minded professor type.

We climbed from the tricar and went into the green building. The inside was not ornate, functional rather, but extremely well kept. The household had retired, and Trobt led me to a room that was obviously a kitchen, except that all equipment had been built into the walls. He served me from dishes that had been left heated, and ate at the same table with me, and in all ways treated me as a guest.

I was too weary to respond well to Trobt's conversation and after we finished our meals he led me to a bedroom, where I slept on a pallet raised high above the floor, as were all their beds.

4

The next morning I expected Trobt to bring up my request for a meeting with the other members of the Council, or at least to question me further, but instead he led me to a side room of his home and showed me his recreation room. It was beautifully laid out with murals of Veldqan wild life on the walls, and swords and glaives crossed between them.

I noted that the swords here, and in Lyagin's office, had been short. Did that have any correlation with the Roman short sword, I wondered. Some believe it was the secret of Rome's conquest of the vast realms of the barbarians, and even some more socially developed countries. With the short sword the Roman soldiers could stand side by side when they fought, while the barbarians needed more room to wield their longer swords. The effect was that an average three Romans faced an average two long-swordsmen. They parried the long swords with their shields, and used their superior individual combat numbers to win their battles. Their success is legend.

The dominating evidence of recreation in the room was the Game board, and large value boards on each end wall. They were electrically wired in such a way that the occupied squares showed in colored lights—with a different color for each contestant.

"If you are willing, I would like another try at beating you," Trobt said, in his invariably polite manner.

"I am quite willing." There was undoubtedly more to the request than the desire to defeat me. He had a deeper motive, and I thought I knew what it was. For a time I debated whether or not it might be wise to let him win, but decided against it. Partly that decision might have been prompted by false pride.

I took a seat at one end of the Games table—I assumed he wanted to play immediately—but Trobt seemed in no hurry to begin. He leaned against the wall to my left, his arms folded across his chest, and his weight resting on one leg. He was making a deliberate attempt to appear casual—and I would have been convinced that he was, except that at his first words the annotator in the back of my brain warned me to be cautious. His questions would not be as casual as he wanted them to appear.

"Having a like nature I can well understand the impulse that brought you here," he said. "The supreme contest. Playing a gambler's hand—with all retreat cut off, knowing that in the end you would die—unless you performed with greater skill than anyone could expect. The admirable temerity of it! And even now—when you have lost, and will die—you do not regret it, I'm certain."

"I'm afraid you're overestimating my courage and underestimating my expectations," I told him, feeling instinctively that this would be a good time to present my arguments again. "I came here because I wanted to reach a better understanding. We feel that an absolutely unnecessary war, with all its grief and chaos, would be foolhardy. And I fail to see your viewpoint. It strikes me as mere obstinacy."

It took him a minute to see through what I was trying to do: throw him on the defensive, to make him angry, and upset the plan of interrogation he had probably prepared with considerable care. For a moment I thought I had succeeded. At my last words he straightened and let his arms drop to his sides. His lips made a slight change then, growing narrower, and his eyes grew bleak. However, his self-control was too rigid to allow a break. He walked to the seat opposite me at the Game board and sat down, and began arranging his pieces on their starting squares.

"The news of your coming is the first topic of conversation in the City," he said, disregarding my taunt, and apparently going ahead with his original conversation plan. "The clans understand that you have come to challenge—one man against a nation. They greatly admire your audacity, and are wagering heavily on how far you will go in the Final Game. Some are wagering that you will go so far that you will join the heroes. It is a great compliment."

"Look," I said, becoming angry and slipping into Earthian, "I don't know whether you consider me a fool or not, but if you think I came expecting to die—that I'm looking forward to it with pleasure—"

He halted me with an idle gesture of one hand. "You deceive yourself if you believe what you say," he commented. "Tell me this, would you have stayed away if you had known how great the risk was to be?"

I was surprised to find that I did not have a ready answer to his question.

"Shall we play?" Trobt asked.

We played three games, Trobt with great skill, employing diversified and ingenious attacks. But he still had that bit too much audacity in his execution.

I could hardly call it a weakness. In most circumstances it would serve him well as a weapon in routing players of lesser or equal skill—or less courage. However, by being aware of his impulsiveness as a potential weakness—and deliberately playing to bring it out—I set him at a disadvantage. I won each time.

"You are undoubtedly a Master," Trobt said, at the end of the third game. "But there is more to it. Would you like me to tell you why I can't beat you?"

"Can you tell me that?" I returned.

"I believe so," he said. "I wanted to try against you again and again, because each time it did not seem that you had defeated me, but only that I had played badly, made childish blunders, that I had lost each game before we ever came to grips. Yet when I entered the duel against you a further time, I'd begin to blunder again."

He shoved his hands more deeply under his weapons belt,

leaning back and observing me with his direct inspection. "My blundering then has to do with you, rather than myself," he said. "Your play is excellent, of course, but there is more beneath the surface than above. This is your talent—you lose the first game to see an opponent's weakness—and play it against him."

I could not deny it. But neither would I concede it. Any small advantage I might hold here would be sorely needed later.

"I understand Humans a little," Trobt said. "Enough to know that very few of them would come to challenge us without some other purpose. They have no taste for death, with glory or without." His gaze was penetrating.

"I believe," he resumed, when I made no reply, "that you came here to challenge in your own way, which is to find any weakness we might have, either in our military or, in some odd way, in our very selves."

Once again, with a minimum of help from me, he had arrived at a correct answer. From here on—against this man— I would have to walk in a narrow line.

"I think," Trobt said more slowly, glancing down at the board between us then back to my expression, "that this may be the *first* Game, and that you are more dangerous than you want us to see, that you are accepting the humiliation of allowing yourself to be thought of as weaker than you are, in actuality. You intend to find our weakness, and somehow you expect to bring to your states what you find."

I looked across at him without expression. He was getting too near to leave me with any great ease. "What weakness do you fear I've seen?" I countered.

"You are not a fool, that I know," Trobt said. "You must by this time have the certainty that you will die. Yet you persist in acting in ways not consistent with that certainty. Which puzzles me. Do you believe that we can be outsmarted, even when you are in a position from which there can be no escape?"

"I would be the fool you suggested if I answered that," I pointed out.

Trobt placed his hands carefully on the board between us, and rose to his feet. Before he could say what he intended a small boy pulling a toy resembling a riding horse came into the room and grabbed Trobt's trouser leg. He was the first blond child I had seen on Veldq.

The boy pointed at the swords on the wall. "Da," he said, beseechingly, making reaching motions. "Da."

Trobt put a fond hand on the boy's shoulder but kept his attention on me. After a moment a faint humorless smile moved his lips. He seemed to grow taller, giving the impression of a strong man remembering his strength. "You will find no weakness to report," he said. He sat down again and placed the child on his lap.

The boy grabbed immediately at a metal ring hanging in Trobt's belt and began playing with it, while Trobt stroked his hair. I had noted earlier that all Veldqans dearly loved children.

"Do you have any idea how many of our ships were used to wipe out your fleet?" Trobt asked abruptly.

As I allowed myself to show the interest I felt he put the boy on the floor and leaned toward me. "One," he said.

I very nearly called Trobt a liar—one ship obliterating a thousand—before I remembered that Veldqans were not liars, and that Trobt was not lying. Somehow this small underpopulated planet had developed a science of weapons that surpassed that of the Ten Thousand Worlds.

I had thought that perhaps my vacation on this Games centered planet would result in some mutual information that would bring quick negotiation, or conciliation, that players of a chess-like game would be easy to approach, that I would meet men intelligent enough to see the absurdity of such an ill-fated war against the overwhelming odds of the Ten Thousand Worlds Federation—intelligent enough to foresee the disaster that would result from such a fight. It began to look as though the disaster might be to the Ten Thousand rather than to the One.

The child continued to play with the ring on Trobt's belt, trying to get his attention. Trobt looked down indulgently and nodded, and rose and began to run, with exaggerated effort, to the delight of the boy who laughed and continued to hold onto the ring, and with its help managing to keep up with Trobt. Somehow, even in this child's play Trobt managed to keep his dignity. It was so much a part of him that probably nothing he could do would lessen it.

When the boy tired Trobt sent him off to play, and sat down again across from me. "I'm not certain whether his love for that running game is an instinct, or merely that we play it so often with him that he was learned to love it," he remarked in partial explanation of his play.

"Why would it be an instinct?" I wondered aloud.

"The dleeth, you understand," Trobt offered in explanation.

"The dleeth?"

"You don't know about them?"

"Very little," I answered. "They were savage beasts, I've heard, and were quite a menace to you Veldqans in the old days."

"They were much more than a menace," Trobt responded. "You might go so far as to say that they shaped our history."

I could see that he had a story to tell, and I waited.

"The dleeths are savage, four-footed, hairy beasts, resembling the big cats of your Earth, but larger and more fierce. And note this—they are intelligent!"

"They must have been formidable adversaries," I led him on.

"So formidable that we would never have been able to survive the struggle, except that they had no hands and could not develop technology. Also, their instincts were purely predatory, while the Veldqans fought with a pride in their race, and its ultimate future, that had always been their first consideration. Yet the struggle went on from our race's earliest memories until a mere few hundred years ago.

"Picture this—" Trobt had warmed to his tale—which I saw was an emotional reaction, despite the fact that the war with the dleeth had been over for so long. "A family would be wakened by the sound of claws gouging the outer wall of their home. They would know what it was—and that their lives were in great danger. If they had had the foresight to prepare an escape tunnel, or were in some other way able to escape, they still never lost the dleeth.

"They could outrun the animals, but the savage beasts never gave up. The chase would go on for days, or even longer, until the dleeth finally caught them, or they were able to reach other clansmen who could help them fight the animals. Usually they had to turn at last and fight for their lives. A single family was seldom a match for even one of the creatures. All over Veldq those struggles went on. For centuries."

"What finally became of the animals?" I found myself very interested.

"With the development of technology, we devised more efficient weapons, and the dleeth were no longer a match for us. Then the chase was reversed, and we hunted them, until now only a few dleeth survive, in the frigid regions of the north, where they had fled. We made no effort to hunt them down."

"I see the purpose of the child's ring," I said. "A young one would hold onto it as the family fled."

"Correct. A family never had more than one child at a time; it would have been impossible to protect more." Trobt paused, himself gripped by the tale that he must have heard and contemplated innumerable times.

"I understand that almost all of the children are born in the City," I prompted.

"In the ancient days the City was the one strong point the dleeth were never able to breach," Trobt answered. "It was held by the Danlee, one of the stronger clans, and there was seldom unity among the clans, yet any family about to bear a child was given sanctuary within its walls.

"The clans were nomads—made so by the aggression of the dleeth—but they always made every effort to reach the City when childbirth was imminent. That is why nearly everyone, except the Kismans, and those from the farthest outlands, regard the City as their homeplace. We have a saying about it: 'All roads take you to Cha-Dan.'"

That sounded similar to a saying used in an early stage of Earth history, and it had meant something important to the people then, but its precise meaning was not something I had heard explained.

We both were silent for a moment, and I took the opportunity to use the twitch code in my tissues to make a note of our conversation on tape. The influence of the dleeth on the Veldqans' history should be important. And if the "all roads..." quotation were reported to an anthropologist, he might get some meaning from it.

Later that evening I walked alone in Trobt's roof garden, deep in consideration of the latest background information I had received on Veldq. The survival of the fittest. That theory had come into question lately, but here it explained much of the physical and temperamental makeup of the Veldqans. The weak and the inefficient had not survived. The present Veldqans would be strong physically and mentally, and by instinct courageous and resourceful, little given to small talk or trivial activities. Was that something that could be exploited? I was not able to name it—as yet.

Walking in Veldq's heavier gravity took more energy than I cared to expend, but too long a period without exercise brought a dull ache to the muscles of my shoulders and the base of my neck.

This was my third week on Veldq, and I had slept at least ten hours each night since I arrived, and found myself exhausted at the day's end, unless I was able to take a nap or lie down during the afternoon.

The flowers and shrubbery in the garden seemed to feel the weight of the gravity also, for most of them grew low, and many sent creepers out along the ground. Overhead, strange formations of stars clustered thickly and shed a glow on the garden very like Earth's moonlight.

I was just beginning to feel the heavy drag in my leg tendons when a woman's voice said, "Why don't you rest awhile." It spun me around, and I searched for the source of the voice.

I found her in a nook in the bushes, seated on a contour chair that allowed her to stretch out in a half-reclining position. She must have weighed near to two hundred fifty Earth-weight pounds.

However, what startled me more than the sound of her voice was that she had spoken in the universal language of the Ten Thousand Worlds. And without accent!

"You're—" I began.

"Human," she finished for me.

"How did you get here?" I asked eagerly.

"With my husband." She was obviously enjoying my bewilderment. She was a beautiful woman, in a gentle bovine way, and very friendly. Her blonde hair was done in tight ringlets.

"You mean—Kalin Trobt?" I asked.

"Yes." As I stood trying to phrase my wonderment into more questions, she asked, "You're the Earthman, aren't you?"

I nodded. "Where did you learn my language?"

"It's my native tongue." I knew a quick delight when she gave the answer I had expected.

"Are you from Earth?"

"No. My home World is Mandel's Planet, in the Thumb Group."

She indicated a fur-covered hassock of a pair, and I seated myself on the lower and leaned an elbow on the higher, beginning to smile. It would have been difficult not to smile in the presence of anyone so contented. "How did you meet Kalin?" I asked.

"It's a simple love story. He visited Mandel's Planet—without revealing his true identity, of course—met, and courted me. I learned to love him, and agreed to go to his world as his wife."

"Did you know that he wasn't. . . . That he—" I stumbled over just how to phrase the question. And wondered if I should have started it.

Her teeth showed white and even as she smiled. She propped a pillow under one plump pretty arm ". . . that he wasn't Human?" I was grateful for the way she put me at ease—almost as though we had been old friends.

I shrugged.

"I didn't know." For a moment she seemed to draw back into her thoughts. "He couldn't tell me. It was a secret he had to keep. When I arrived here and learned that his planet wasn't a charted World, was not even Human, I was a little uncertain and lonesome. But not frightened. I knew Kalin would never let me be hurt. Even my loneliness left quickly. Kalin and I love each other very deeply. I couldn't be more happy than I am now."

She seemed to see I did not consider that my question had been fully answered. "You're wondering still if I mind that he isn't Human, aren't you?" she asked. "Why should I? After all, what does it mean to be 'Human'? It is only a word that differentiates one race of people from another. I seldom think of the Veldqans as being different—and I certainly never feel that they're beneath me."

"Does it bother you—if you'll pardon this curiosity of mine—that you will never bear Kalin's children?"

"The child you saw this morning is my son," she answered complacently.

"But that's impossible," I blurted.

"Is it?" she asked. "You saw the proof."

"I'm no expert at that sort of thing," I said slowly, "but I've always understood that the possibility of two separate races producing offspring was millions to one."

"Greater than that, probably," she agreed. "But whatever the odds, sooner or later the number was bound to come up. This was it."

I shook my head, but there was no arguing a fact. "Wasn't it a bit unusual that Kalin didn't marry a Veldqan woman?"

"He has married—two of them," she answered. "I'm his third wife." She laughed merrily at my expression, and I realized only then that she was obviously happy to talk with someone from the Ten Thousand Worlds.

"Then they do practice polygamy," I said. "Are you content with such a marriage?"

"Oh, yes," she answered. "You see, besides being very much loved, I occupy a rather enviable position here. I, ah—" She grew slightly flustered. "Well, the other women—the Veldqan women—can bear children only once every eight years, and during the other seven—" She hesitated again, obviously embarrassed, but she laughed and went resolutely on.

"During the other seven, they lose their feminine appearance, and don't think of themselves as women. While I—" Her glance dropped. "I am always of the same sex, as you might say, always a woman. My husband is the envy of all his friends."

As I was learning another facet of this culture, one of its basics, I listened eagerly.

After her first reticence the woman—Darlene, she said her name was—talked freely, and I reaped a harvest of information.

I learned the answer to the riddle of the boy-girls of Veldq. And at least one reason for their great affection for children. One year of fertility in eight. . . .

Once again I saw the imprint of the voracious dleeth on this people's culture. In their age-old struggle with their sub-temperate climate, and its short growing seasons—and more particularly with the dleeth—the Veldq women had been shaped by evolution to fit their environment better. The women's strength could not be spared for frequent childbearing, therefore it had been limited. Further, one small child could be carried, or an older one aided, in the frequent flights from the dleeth, but no more than one could be cared for. Nature had done its best to cope with the problem. In the seven off years she tightened the women's flesh, atrophying glands and organs—making them nonfunctional—and changing their bodies to be more fit to labor and survive—and to fight, if necessary. It was an excellent adaptation—for a time and environment where a low birth rate was an asset to survival.

However, this adaptation had left only a narrow margin for race perpetuation. Each woman could bear only four children in her lifetime. That, I realized, as we talked, was the reason why the Veldqans had not colonized other planets, even though they had space flight—and why they probably never would, without a drastic change in their biological makeup. That left so little ground for a quarrel between them and the Federation. Yet here we were, poised to spring into a death struggle. The sheer futility of it was nauseating.

What of the Veldqans today, was my next thought. That survival asset was no longer necessary, now that the dleeth had been all but eliminated. It could only be a drag on the culture—and a social tinder pot. That I would have to consider and investigate, if possible, at length in the near future.

We had talked for a considerable time more, until I grew weary—as did the woman, I saw as I glanced at her. "You are a very unusual person, in a very unusual position. I hope that you will always be as happy as you are today."

"Thank you," she accepted my good wishes. She made a motion to rise. "I hope you enjoy your visit with us. And that I will see you again before you return to Earth."

I saw then that she did not know of my peculiar position

in her home. I wondered if she knew even of the threat of war between us and her adopted people. I decided not, or she would surely have spoken of it. Either Trobt had deliberately avoided telling her, perhaps to spare her the pain it would have caused, or she had noted that the topic of my presence was disturbing to him and had tactfully refrained from inquiring.

It was evident, also, that she knew nothing of my imminent death. For just an instant I wondered if I should explain everything to her, and have her use the considerable influence she must have with Trobt. I dismissed the idea as unworthy—and useless. Even in this Trobt would never compromise, and I would only be causing dissension between them.

I never did ask Trobt for details of the Final Game. There would be little point. No matter how much I knew about it, in the end I would die. I preferred to let the Game come as something unknown.

Conversely, I never discouraged Trobt from talking about it. I would show as little timidity as possible. Once he spoke of it at some length while we walked in his gardens.

"The near prospect of entering the Final Game, I would imagine, must heighten a man's awareness of all about him," he said. "I do not know if he would see everything more clearly, or whether he would merely see things differently, because of his inner condition. Perhaps a bit of both. Certainly everything he observed would be colored by it."

Again the puzzlement of this man. Here he was, the epitomical leader of a warrior nation, who should have been by nature extroverted, but yet introspective and open to discussion.

He waited for no return comment from me. "It would be a time to sum up his philosophy, to review his life, and decide which of his past decisions had been right and which wrong. That last would be difficult. I suppose the most he could ask was that he had followed his personal philosophy to the best of his ability—even though he might never have put it into words."

My own philosophy, I reflected, would probably be summed up best by a quotation from Kant: *Recognize the big things as*

*big and the small things as small, and laugh in the face of the
inevitable.*

I might have spent some time reflecting on that except that
Trobt was still speaking. "Then there is the decision he must
make on how he will conduct himself in his final test. Will
he give it his best efforts—knowing that that best can have only
the same inevitable result? Or will he decide to lose early? To
avoid the trial and pain, and end the stress before his last
reserve of moral stamina is gone, and he is left a coward in
the eyes of his fellow men who watch?

"Strangely enough, something about you," Trobt continued, "has aroused an empathy in me that I have never felt
before, even when former friends faced the tests." He mused,
almost to himself. "Perhaps I should guard against that feeling.
I'm convinced by now that you are a man whom other men
instinctively like. My allowing it to affect me could very well
hinder me in the task I must perform."

His words brought a new realization: Trobt, being so personally involved in the drama taking place here, had indeed
let himself be carried further emotionally than was best for his
side.

It was not so much affection for me but, as he had said,
empathy. Apparently our natures were so nearly alike that he
could not observe me with the necessary objectivity; everything
that happened to me, every nuance of my situation here, passed
through the screen guarding his emotional makeup, and he
suffered with my every anxiety and anguish. He was like a
parent who says sincerely, "This hurts me more than it does
you." Right at that moment I would have liked the help of a
competent psychoanalyst to study him further.

Did that empathy present a way for me to win here? At first
thought it seemed unworthy—as my thought of having Trobt's
wife intercede for me had been—but it was not only I who
was involved here. Greater weight must be given to my fellow
Humans.

Further, despite any involvement Trobt was experiencing,
he thus far had not let it keep him from his duty. He was using
every means he knew to extract useful information from me,
in total disregard of any pain it might bring me—and I was

certain he would continue to do so, without any ethical or moral qualms.

I had found a weakness in him—should I be any less pragmatic than he?

It was a matter I would have to explore more deeply, as quickly as possible.

"I have always felt," Trobt soon began again, "that a man, to prove himself, must give the last iota of his skill and strength in the Final Game. That the man who quit before he had to was craven. Now I see it differently, and I have lost much of that certainty. Perhaps the man I considered a coward had seen the test in the new light I mentioned, perhaps he had a new wisdom, perhaps he saw then something I did not see.

"I do know that I have never pitied a man so much as I have those who fought the hardest. Who fought up to and beyond their strength—until they broke. Then they had nothing left with which to hold up their pride. Some stood and cried—strong men, I knew—some ran, and others begged to be spared. I was sick with their humiliation."

I did not need to hear this from Trobt to make my choice. Despite the influence of his words. I had already decided that I would give the best I had in the Final Game, but that above all else, I would die like a man. They would never see me crawl or beg. This was my own determination, apart from consideration of how my behavior would reflect on the Human race. It was something that had to be done. For the first time I had a clear understanding of Trobt's 'yag loogt'n'balt. I *must* fight.

Also, however, I recognized fear. Fear of the breaking of spirit he had mentioned. Back on Earth I had had a very dear friend who had died of the one form of cancer that science had never been able to conquer. My friend was as courageous a man as I have ever known. When he learned that he had contracted the fatal disease he had not complained. He faced the coming end without flinching, and bore its steadily increasing pain certainly better than I could have done. But as the final crisis grew nearer, as the continual, agonizing torture persisted, and increased, as his mind grew less coherent, I watched his distress tear something out of his spirit. The hard

core of courage which he had possessed before was gone, and
he had nothing left with which to fight. He was not the same
man he had been before. What he had been was no longer
there. When they touched him then to move him he cried for
them to be gentle, and complained of their carelessness. He
would not eat because of the pain. Between spasms of agony—
that drugs could no longer hold back—tears of self-pity would
flow from his eyes, and he would beg us, his impotent friends,
to help him. The place Trobt had touched was still raw from
the memory of him. Could I hope to be any stronger?

"It is an awful thing to observe a man whose heart has died
before his body," Trobt concluded. "I doubt whether one is
doing a man a kindness to warn him in advance of the time
of the Final Game. Perhaps it is better to wait until the last
minute. I do not know. I suppose it depends on the man."

I recognized only then that he had been speaking Earthian.
For a moment I wondered why. Then a second thought intruded. The whole tenor of his talk had held an overtone of
sadness. Was he trying to say something to me? Or ask me
something? Could he mean...?

I turned sharply to face him. Perhaps he read fright in my
eyes. For I saw pity in his eyes as he nodded.

"It begins tomorrow," he said.

5

The night after Trobt informed me that I was to undergo the Final Game I slept only the last few hours before dawn. The first hours after retiring I spent recording the events of the day on the nerve tape. I had difficulty restraining myself from recording reactions that were merely the result of my own emotional overcharge. And that I wanted very much not to do.

Because—I was ashamed to admit it, even to myself—I was morbidly afraid. The certainty that I would die before the Final Game was over was more than I could face with steady nerves.

And yet it was purely a physical reaction. My mind was, if not unafraid, calm. Mentally I was satisfied that my life had been a good one. It had been stimulating, with perhaps more peaks of pleasure and enjoyment than the average man experienced. If I died now I could not feel cheated. I was very nearly content. But my body. . . .

My body persisted in exuding a cold perspiration that clung to the bed covering as I turned restlessly. My bowels forced me to make frequent trips to the lavatory, and each time I rose I detected a faint odor of fear that made me want to retch in self-disgust.

I knew that only a stupid man has no fear, yet I violently resented my inability to maintain its control over my body and its functioning. I no longer felt one with it, and watched it as would a stranger who stood at my side. When I moved, it was as though I were operating a machine with rigid mechanical controls. And as the night wore on the numbness in my body washed up a wave of black despair into my brain. When I was able to think at all coherently it was with a desperate effort to find a way to escape the ordeal before me.

Father, if it be thy will. . . .

By the next morning my bodily dysfunction was gone, but it was replaced by an emotional frigidity. I felt drained of sensation, and dry as old paper that crumbles at a touch.

As I met Trobt and we walked toward the tricar tunnel, I noted without caring the three guardsmen who fell into step with us. On the active level of my mind I was thinking of—nothing. The annotator in the corner of my skull alone was observing everything about me. But then it always did.

It watched and made note of every speech and action of Trobt and the guardsmen, their reactions to me, whether favorable, unfavorable, embarrassed, uneasy, or whether concealed or unreadable. Likewise, it set down any reaction of one to the other, briefly marking down smiles, gestures, and significant voice tones.

I realized with surprise that it had not accepted my fate—it intended to escape!

Yet personally I felt and showed no reaction to anything I observed. Even to myself I never specified any response to the words and expressions of those around me, merely letting them silently take their place in the memory banks of the annotator.

"Pardon." Trobt's word broke into my mental paralysis. "I've forgotten my side piece." He smiled stiffly. "It is a weakness of vanity, perhaps," he said, "but I am undressed without it." He turned and retraced his steps.

As we waited a guard flexed his shoulder irritably and pulled at an arm strap. He spoke something to a second guard I couldn't hear. The other helped him make an adjustment on the strap. The third guard watched idly. For just an instant all three were turned away from me—and I reacted.

As I moved I did not know exactly what I intended, I knew only that the annotator had summed up the total of trivia about me—and arrived at a decision. With that kind of auxiliary mind the last possible moment is the right time to address a situation so as not to be hampered by earlier decisions fitted to a half-understanding of upcoming action.

An opening to a side hall was only a few feet away, and I stepped quickly around its corner. To the spring door of a disposal chute.

Holding the door back with a shoulder I kicked once and I was inside and sliding down a surface made slick by the juices of discarded refuse.

For an instant a small doubt irked at my mind. Had the escape been too easy? Something like the single opening I had left Trobt in the second Game? If the man learned as rapidly and efficiently as I had seen him do in small things. . . . Was he playing the Game with me? Or, a second thought. . . . Had his empathy with me led him to allow me to escape?

I decided against either. Very likely the thought that I might try to escape and take refuge in the City hadn't occurred to him. And if I were wrong, and he had planned this—for a purpose I could not see—I might turn my freedom to my own advantage. And finally, what did I have to lose?

I could not stop my descent but after a few hurried experiments found that I could slow it by pressing my hands and knees against the sides of the chute. Despite this I hit the water with velocity enough to carry me well under.

I came up into almost complete darkness. The odor around me was foul, and unsavory chunks of garbage bumped against my face and body.

I made no effort to swim, letting the locked air in my clothing keep me afloat, while I kept my head above water and let the current carry me along. I rounded a bend and ahead could see the dim light of an opening. With slow easy strokes I guided myself toward it.

I stayed under Hearth for two days. At first I had intended to go out through the breach in the wall that served as an exit for the river that flowed beneath its ramparts—River Widd, it was called—but decided against it. Out in the open they could easily hunt me down, while this made a perfect hiding place. I fully expected them to send men down to hunt for me, but

I saw readily that it would be an almost impossible task for them to find me. Most of the vast underground was in near darkness and its innumerable foundations, pillars, mud and garbage flats, and disposal exits would require an army to explore thoroughly.

The first several hours of freedom I took the risk of shedding my heavy cloak and clothing and spreading them in the sun that came in through a gap in the wall. When they were passably dry I put them on again and crawled back into the darkness. I found a semi-dry spot high on a mud bank, and waited. My heavy cloak held off most of the cold, and I was not too uncomfortable.

There was no sign of pursuit during the morning and twice I napped. Late in the day the sound of dripping water, perhaps fifty yards to my right, reminded me that I was thirsty. I crawled to the spot from which the sound had come and found a leak in a pipe that brought water into the city. I caught the dripping water in my hands and drank my fill.

For all of the two days and nights under the city I stayed near the leaking pipe, with water my only sustenance. The nights were miserably cold and even my cloak could not keep me warm. Each morning I crawled back to my sunny spot and allowed the warmth to creep back into my flesh.

By the third morning I knew I could wait no longer. I had to have food, and a better place to sleep. I had explored the part of the underground made visible by the light from the gap and found a stairway leading up to the city. They might be expecting me at the top, but it was a chance I had to take.

No one waited for me as I came out of the passageway. The most dangerous part was over.

My chances of remaining free should not be too bad, I decided. I looked enough like the Veldqans to pass easily as one of them, and securing my needs would not be difficult.

I stopped at a street stall a short distance from the ramp exit with just the semblance of a plan in mind. One of the reasons I had stayed the two days underground was to give my beard time to grow. It was tough and dark and the two days had brought a short but thick stubble. It was a bit skimpy as a beard, but in a few days it would be quite passable.

The main difficulty was that though many of the Veldqan men wore beards, they covered only the ridges of the jaws and neck fronts. For some reason hair did not grow on their cheeks. While on mine, of course, it did. This apparently small difference would make me quite conspicuous. I had rubbed a handful of dirt on my cheeks, hoping it would hide the whiskers.

I bought a knife sharp enough to be used as a razor, toilet articles, food, and a change of clothing, and paid for them by signing a name to a blue slip. These slips would be the Veldqans' best chance of tracing me.

I had learned their money system even before my first business with Iten. A Veldqan reaching adulthood served one year in the public services, as clerk, maintenance worker, electrician, or others. At the end of the service period he was free to seek another occupation. Until he was able to find it he was permitted to obtain his needs by the simple process of signing his name to the blue script in the amount of his purchase. If he was unable to redeem the scripts before they reached a certain maximum he simply returned to the public services for another year. After which he began again. Credit was established by depositing slips acquired from others. I do not know if the system would be adequate in a larger unit of government, but here it worked quite well.

There was a military that one could join, if he preferred that to civil service, but the military was a harshly disciplinary life, and I understood that not many selected it as a temporary occupation.

Most of those entering the military chose it as a career. After approximately ten years of service they were eligible to compete in the Games, and those with high scores entered the executive ranks of the City's government. They still retained their army rank, but their actual service was mainly honorary. I believe that was the post held by Trobt, and the other authorities of Hearth. That was about the limit of information I had received thus far on that portion of their lives.

Most Veldqans were psychologically incapable of falsehood, and there was very little cheating with the blue script—until ˙ came into contact with the system. The names I used on the ˙ would not be registered and quite probably the authorities

would readily guess their source. It would have been wiser for
me to use the name of an actual citizen of the City—but I
couldn't quite bring myself to do it. Somewhere, as the saying
went, a man has to draw his line.

I intended to limit my purchases to necessities, and perhaps
it would take time for the slips to go through the bookkeeping
routine.

I debated whether or not to take possession of a tricar and
get as far as possible from the sector of the city where the search
would most likely center, but decided that the tricar might be
another way to trace me. Sooner or later I would have to
abandon it. It would be wiser to walk. Hearth's ramparts
stretched along the River Widd for probably a dozen miles.
I could reach the center on foot without difficulty.

Just off Hearth's central market I found a sleeping place.
I had to pay nothing for the quarters, they were free for the
taking. The room on the third floor was neat and well cared
for, and when I wandered downstairs found that meals were
served free also. Was this a part of Veldq's welfare system? And
how much more was there to it? That did not seem too per-
tinent to my task here, and I didn't pursue it further, being
content with the aid it gave me. For the time being I was safe,
and grateful for the rest I so badly needed.

The following day I did not go out at all. I wanted to give
my beard an opportunity to grow, and more importantly, I
needed to weigh my situation, and if possible plan future
moves.

Now that I had time to view my escape without the pressure
of sudden decision, I decided that there was much to be hopeful
about—despite the handicaps I would still have. True, there
was small possibility that I could remain free for any great
length of time. Eventually they would find me, by tracing the
blue money, or through errors I was bound to make. Then I
would probably have the choice of forcing them to kill me
immediately or awaiting the time of their pleasure.

However, I intended to make good use of my time until
then. My primary objective was to learn more of the workings
of the Veldqan society, and to find a power source to send my
twitch-tape report back to the Worlds.

My fear was completely gone by this time. When I searched for a reason I was astounded by what I saw. I had already counted myself a dead man, and there is little that can frighten a man who has resigned himself to death. With it also I discovered that I had acquired an additional weapon—desperation. A desperation that would make me all the more deadly if I had to fight.

Before I left my room I took the precaution of shaving my cheeks with the knife-razor I had bought, and was confident I could pass as a Veldqan. I left my room then, and wandered through Hearth's wide streets, taking in everything I observed. The rose-pink buildings I saw then were crowded close together, and interspersed with high, ornately carved edifices with pointed turrets. Religious temples, I wondered?

I learned soon to keep close to the edges of the thoroughfares, as did the citizens, alert for tricars careening—out of control, it seemed to me—down the streets. There were no sidewalks, and pedestrians apparently were expected to yield to the vehicles. I quickly grew accustomed to darting out of the way, flattening myself against the buildings bordering the road, and even pulling in my stomach when it seemed certain I would be struck otherwise. Walking there, I decided, was extremely dangerous, yet I never did see a pedestrian hit.

All about the City was an air of cloaked mystery, heightened greatly by the silence. The tricars made no noise, and the citizens all seemed to hurry, as though on some urgent errand. Even the few children I saw were quiet, seeming out of their element in the street, hurrying to some inner refuge. Yet none of the citizens appeared cowed or apprehensive. I was certain there was no repression here, merely the normal repressed nature of the inhabitants.

Very early the fourth day the stark savagery that was so much a part of the Veldqan temperament was brought vividly to my attention.

I had left my room at the break of day, to scout the city, and to find if I could the source of power that supplied Hearth. Or the factories where their implements of war were manufactured. It would be worth more than my life to learn the secret of their superior weapon, or weapons.

Only a short block from the central marketplace I came to the wooden wall of a temporary storage building. On it hung the still bleeding carcass of a man!

He had been lifted until his feet cleared the ground and a short-bladed knife—probably his own—driven through his throat and buried into the boards behind him. The knife had entered at the base of the throat, sharp edge upward, and the weight of the body had forced the blade through the flesh and tendons until it came to rest against the bone of the jaw.

Beside the head—obviously in the victim's own blood—was scrawled: COWARD.

The poor wretch had evidently violated some taboo, and had not had the courage to defend himself. On Veldq a man without courage was a man without Honor—capital H—and without Honor, not fit to live. There would be no attempt to punish the man or men who had killed him.

Honor. On that word, and their conception of it, the Veldqans hung their right to live—much as they had hanged this poor brute with his own knife.

For my own safety, I reflected ruefully, it would be well to keep that Honor concept closely in mind.

I found the City's powerhouse without difficulty—I thought. It was located at the edge of the Citadel where the River Widd entered. I did not risk an entry but searched unobtrusively for outside leads.

Either they were buried or the Veldqans had a different method of transmission than I sought, for I found none. Darkness was creeping in by that time and I decided to return the next day. If I still did not find a way to tap the power by then I would look for wiring beneath the wall. However, I would put that off until the last, I decided, for it would involve a time-consuming search, and the place was so dreary and unclean that I had an aversion to returning.

In all my wandering I found no evidence of their factories, or a weapons technology. There was much of the City that I had not yet covered, and I would do that, but I felt that I would not find them in Hearth.

The probability was that every citizen knew where the weapons were made—but how was I to learn it? I couldn't simply ask. My not knowing would, itself, arouse suspicion. A better method would be to steer a casual conversation around to the subject. But I dared not enter into any extended conversation. My accent alone would give me away. It had been safe enough before they had known of my existence: then they had probably marked it as the way of speaking of an outlander clansman. But word of my escape must have reached most of the citizens by this time, and my speech would give me away quickly. For the same reason I decided not to risk visiting Iten again.

I found a free room in a different section of the market district the next day. I wanted to leave a cold trail for any pursuers. After I'd had a long nap I wandered the streets in my usual pattern, only erratically moving in the direction of the power station. For some unknown reason I had a hunch that I would have no success there, and was in no hurry to reach it.

As I passed a melon-merchant's stall, the old fellow directed an off-slant eye in my direction and motioned with his head, and when I walked over to him he inquired courteously if I would care to join him in a no-stakes Game. It was his slack period, he explained, and he would appreciate my indulgence. I was constantly amazed at how deeply engrossed all the citizens were with the Game. It reminded me fondly of a girl I had courted in my youth, named Marvel. She had loved dancing so much that I never had to wonder how I was to entertain her, I merely chose good places to dance, and kept her quite happy.

The merchant couldn't have recognized me or he would already have registered alarm, I decided, and accepted his invitation. I still had much to learn, and so few sources of information.

I feigned a sore throat, touching my neck gingerly, and murmured a few scratchy words in accepting his offer. He then carried the burden of the conversation as we played, while I restricted myself to leading questions, being as careful as possible not to be too obvious, and remembering to speak hoarsely.

My immediate need was more information on the city, to aid me in my secret survey, and to further my search for a power outlet. Trobt had explained some of the background, and Darlene had helped, but there was much more I needed to know. The merchant readily answered my questions; he was a loquacious man and happy to oblige.

Hearth, the impregnable fortress, the Heart City, he began, was held by the Danlee in ancient days. They were ruled by Miklas of Danlee, a wise and foresighted chieftain, and they grew strong and conquered other tribes. Miklas, when he defeated his foes, gave them the choice of leaving their sons enemies of the Danlee—and therefore prisoners to be slain, or slaves to be used as animals, spent and allowed to die—or using their absolute parental authority and swearing them to eternal fealty to the Danlee, allowing them to be adopted into the Hearth of the Danlee as sons and brothers, to be treated as kin and to expect and own all gentleness of kin to each of the Danlee and the adopted of the Danlee.

Though the principles of honor and vengeance stood high, life of children and respect for strength stood higher, and few parents refused to give their children to the Danlee.

Therefore all the clansmen of Veldq, except the Kismans, and a few savage tribes not worth the conquest, call themselves sons of the Danlee, and the Danlee Citadel their Hearth and the home of their fathers, in the sense that Father means the protector and commander of their children. All this was quite informative, but there still remained much to learn.

The next day I visited a zoo. The only zoo in Hearth, though it contained only one animal. A dleeth.

I had heard rumors that one was being kept in the City, as a curiosity, and I made a point, with my usual discreet inquiries, to find it.

The beast was confined in an area about an acre in size, comprised of a small rocky hill with a shelter at its top, scattered tree and vine clusters, a large patch of green grass covering the far half, and a moat surrounding it all.

Several minutes passed before I was able to locate the dleeth. It was resting in a glass tunnel at the base of the hill—and watching me.

When it saw that I had found it, it rose leisurely and came out of its tunnel, and stood arrogantly, disdainfully, just beneath me, and I noted that it had the topaz eyes of a gila monster. I'm certain it recognized that I was different from its usual visitor.

The animal's white fur should have made it resemble a polar bear, but it was larger, standing a good six feet at the shoulders, and its neck was longer and thinner, with legs that at first glance appeared spindly, but which carried the large body with a springy ease.

It was looking up at me then, with none of the easy hate of Earth's carnivora, but with, I saw, the same curiosity as I had.

From the moment our gazes met I experienced a reaction that was almost distress. The phenomenon of seeing intelligence in those beast eyes was like a pressure beating at my brain. I dismissed it with an effort.

Could the brute speak, I wondered. I had never thought to ask Trobt. Somewhere I had read that intelligence could not develop without a vocabulary. I had never properly considered whether or not I agreed with the theory.

More as a retreat from those curious, disconcerting eyes than because I expected any reply, I called down, "Can you talk?"

Its only response was a flicker of the topaz eyes that must have been scorn. I retreated into silent discomfort. Could an animal be doing this to me, I thought, in mild dismay.

The creature loped over to a huge rock just to my right and stood on its hind legs, and exposing metallic, prehensile claws, raked them down the rock, gouging out a deep track with each claw.

The strength displayed was stupenduous. I had an amused realization then:

The beast was showing off!

I made to leave soon after—my curiosity had been satisfied, and there was nothing more to learn here—when something remarkable occurred. The dleeth came hurrying back to the wall where I stood, and gazed up at me. It made a sound in its throat that was between a groan and a child's cry—and abruptly I was aware of a new realization:

The beast was displaying an abysmal loneliness!

I left the zoo with a kind of incredible wonder at the pity I felt for a creature I knew to be so ferocious and vicious.

6

For some reason I could not explain I did not return to the power station that day, merely continuing my wanderings about the city. And that evening as I was returning to my room I came near to disaster.

A cold wind had come in suddenly from the north, bringing snow and sleet, not quite a storm, but very uncomfortable. I do not know how unusual this was for the early fall season, but I cared for it not at all.

I was striding with my head lowered against the wind, and paying little attention to what went on around me. Brittle bits of sleet riding the wind stung my face, bringing tears to my eyes, and increasing my discomfort. I was looking forward to my warm room when a hard shoulder struck my head and knocked me into the middle of the roadway.

I looked up. "What—" I began.

The man with whom I had collided stood perhaps three paces from me, with his legs spread wide and his lips pulled back from his teeth. He was short and thick, with a hard-lined face and a permanent scowl. The typical Veldqan traits of impetuousness and audacity showed in his expression, betraying a nature obviously cantankerous.

"Your forgiveness," I murmured, and made to pass him and go on.

He reached out a hairy hand and gripped my cloak where it met at the throat. "You would run?" he asked gently.

The moment he spoke I understood why I was being challenged. I had been walking on the wrong side of the road. To do that on Veldq exposed ignorance; to do it and jostle another going the correct way is an insult. I did not know whether or not an apology would be accepted, but I made a try. "I beg you to forgive a stupid one," I said. "I was not properly observant."

The Veldqan had a tinderbox temper. Instead of replying he dug his other hand into my cloak and jerked, with all the weight of his body behind it. The unexpectedness of the action caught me unprepared, and he swung me around until my head struck the wall of a building at the edge of the road.

A scattering of pedestrians collected around us, commenting excitedly and asking questions. Others came running up to join them. I spotted the face of a boy-girl that I recognized, but had no opportunity to dwell on it then.

My assailant still held his grip at my throat. He freed one hand then and drew a short-bladed knife. "He tried to run!" he shouted over his shoulder at the absorbed onlookers. His voice was harsh with excitement—pleased excitement.

"Kill him!" several of the spectators shouted back.

The blow had momentarily dazed me, but now my head cleared and I saw that the time for apologies had passed. I made ready to meet the man's next move.

A tall bearded Veldqan in the uniform of the military shouldered his way through the crowd. "What is happening here?" he asked.

The onlookers quieted instantly. The military act as police in the City, and citizens show them strict respect—with good cause. Anyone opposing them in their duties is automatically assigned to the Final Game.

"He tried to run," the short man at my side said. His face had taken on a bone hardness, and his voice was wicked and quiet.

The officer raised inquiring eyebrows at me. I noted that the short man had not had to state my offense, the accusation that I had tried to run summed up the situation to the officer's complete satisfaction.

There was nothing left but to fight. "The gentleman has misconceived, Guardian," I said, giving him his formal address of rank. "Will you be kind enough to indicate the offending party?"

Several of the first men to reach us gave their version of what had happened, the short man gave his, and the guardian turned to me. "I am prepared to give him satisfaction," I said, disdaining to argue.

The guardian found the short man to be the injured party. That gave him the choice of weapons.

"The short knife," he said, unhesitatingly.

The Veldqans live with their short knives. They use them in games, contests, hunting, and some even for eating. I'd have little chance fighting such a one with the unfamiliar weapon.

The guardian turned to me. "Conditions?" he asked.

The annotator, as usual, had been busy. "Blindfold us," I said firmly.

I surprised myself as much as our onlookers. I sought to explain my choice, and quickly came up with the answer. Somewhere I had read a novel of Earth's historical past in which a man with no proficiency with weapons was challenged to a meeting by a skilled duelist. He had chosen blindfolds and pistols. He had found an equalizer.

There was a moment of silence around us, then shouts of approval. Variety lent savor to a contest, apparently. The guardian nodded his consent. My opponent was allowed no protest.

The boy-girl I had noted at the edge of the crowd—she was the worker I had seen briefly in Lyagin's office—stepped forward and tore strips of cloth from her cloak lining and handed them to the guardian. I knew by her expression that she was very much on my side.

The guardian bound the strips of cloth about our eyes. He had evidently been considering the aspects of our contest, for now he said, "To insure proper opportunity for each I will call 'now' at regular intervals. You will then make a sound audible to your opponent." He turned to the spectators. "You will keep the silence until the contest is completed." They obeyed instantly.

This, I knew, would be no fight decided by the mere drawing of blood. The Veldq code demanded the death or complete disability of at least one of the fighters. I recalled then that even that might not be the end: if the loser did not die, he was expected to take his own life. A grim outlook indeed.

I would have to put aside any thoughts of showing mercy should I gain an advantage. Doing that would consign me to death as quickly as refusing to fight would have done. I'd have to kill him, if I could.

Someone put a knife in my hand, and took me by the arm and led me a few paces backward. As I stood waiting for the signal I pushed my knife into my belt and tugged the heavy cloak from my shoulders. I wrapped it around my left forearm, where it made a thick bundle. I heard a murmur run through the crowd. It must have been approval for there was no protest.

The guardian barked, "Now!" and I took the short knife in my right hand, and shifted three quick strides to my left. I heard my opponent grunt—I judged about fifteen feet away— and I whistled sharply. A whistle is more difficult to locate exactly than the sound of a voice.

Three times we answered the guardian's signal, and each time the short man's reply came from a different area. After my first move I held my position. Remembering what I had heard of Veldq knife fighting I knew that their favorite stroke is an uppercut that eviscerates an opponent and rips up through the belly muscles. The gruesome remains probably gave satisfaction to the winner's machismo spirit. I bent slightly, with my cloak arm across the top of my legs.

The short man's third call came from a mere two paces to my right. I had deliberately waited for him to sound first, and now I whistled, and whirled to face him.

I had judged correctly!

I heard a small scuffle of pebbles as he sprang forward, and felt the savage thrust of a knife blade as it went through the fabric of my cloak and buried its point in the flesh of my forearm.

At the instant the blade struck I brought my right arm around, overhand, and felt my knife bury itself in flesh.

My opponent made a strangling sound, and jerked back as I pulled my knife free. His had stayed buried where it had stuck in my arm.

"It is over," the guardian said. The crowd around us began to cheer.

I removed the knife from my arm and jerked off my blindfold. My late opponent, I saw, was still on his feet, unmoving, standing with blank wonder on his face. I stepped over to him and put one arm around his waist.

He had lost his blindfold in our scuffle, and I noted that his features were slack and lackluster, with all their color gone. The harshness had left them also. He looked up at me, and tried to speak, but his face twisted with pain, and he began to cough, and could not stop. His legs gave beneath him, and he pulled me down with him, and both of us sat on the ground. My arm was still around him, and his head rested in my lap.

His coughing eased off, but he still did not seem to understand what had happened. He passed his tongue over dry lips, but failed to moisten them. "Something is going on inside that is wrong," he mumbled, and closed his eyes.

I turned to the crowd around us. "This man needs help," I called. "Give me a hand, please."

No one moved, all the faces about me seemed, not unconcerned, but puzzled. As though they did not understand my words.

I turned to the guardian. "Won't you help him?" I asked.

I drew nearer. "What would be the purpose?" he asked. He was as puzzled as the others.

"If we don't stop this bleeding, he'll die," I declared.

"Yet if we save his life, he will have to kill himself as soon as he is able," the guardian reasoned with me. "Would that be better?"

I couldn't simply let the man die, yet I suspected that more argument here would be wasted. I turned to the boy-girl. "Will you help me?" I asked.

She knelt beside us, and picking up one of our discarded knives, cut away the hurt man's leather blouse, exposing his wounded shoulder. Blood ran from the wound in a steady stream.

"It's an artery," she said, looking at me inquiringly. She too seemed not to understand why I was asking for her help.

It did look as though we were too late, but I had to be certain. "Bind it," I ordered, gathering in the two blindfolds, that had fallen near us, and handing them to her.

She folded one blindfold two times and put it over the wound, and pressed the other tight across it, and bound the ends.

By this time blood had begun to run from one corner of his mouth and into my lap.

At that moment the man opened his eyes and looked directly at me. "I don't understand what's going on around here," he said very distinctly. His eyes slowly closed.

The guardian bent down and checked his pulse, and afterward raised one eyelid. "This man has died," he announced.

Dear God, no, I thought. I had never killed a man before.

This blind, stupid, pointless savagery.

It took a minute for me to come out of my semi-shock, as I considered the implications. Was this the difference between the two races? The quality of mercy in one, and the sheer incomprehensibility of it in the other? Was one right and the other wrong, or was one weak and the other strong? It was not something I had the depth of wisdom to decide. I rose and began to walk away.

A small warm hand slipped into mine and I turned and saw the boy-girl looking up at me, her eyes bright with excitement—and I swear it—adoration. "A dleeth!" she exclaimed.

It was impossible to remain unmoved before her admiration and I felt my morbid mood lift slightly, though still weighted by the reproach of my conscience. "What is your name?" I asked.

"Yasi," she answered, making a pretense of pouting because I had not known it.

I remembered well how she had looked at me in Lyagin's office, and I was as happy to see her then as though she had been an old friend.

My happier mood was interrupted by the guardian, who had placed himself in front of me, and who now asked, "What is your contingent?"

I stood for an instant, puzzled. Until Yasi pulled at my cloak and turned me half away from the guardian. "He wants to know your contingent in the military," she said aloud, then in a voice not audible to the guardian explained, "Your beard. Only the military wear them."

My small knowledge of this society had trapped me again. It was inevitable that it would happen, consistently. What I should do then escaped me.

Yasi saw my bewilderment, and knowing my dilemma, improvised quickly. "In the beginning of the scuffle with his opponent his head was struck against a building wall with severe force," she said. "I fear that it has left him with small use of his senses."

The guardian smiled and nodded, quite obviously humoring her. "That is quite possible," he agreed.

"He is a personal friend of mine," Yasi continued her improvisation. "I would be gratified if he would be placed in my care."

"It is not permitted," the guardian answered. "He must be interviewed by an officer of superior rank."

"I am Yasi, of the Lyagin clan, daughter of Lyagin, records administrator of Hearth." Yasi, I saw, was putting all the pressure she knew on the guardian. "I will vouch for his safe conduct."

The soldier smiled indulgently, and made no answer, merely placing his hand on my arm and leading me away.

"See that his wound is treated quickly!" Yasi shouted after us, in frustration. I knew by her voice that she was crying.

I was grateful for her effort, and by reading between the lines knew that she had gone further than was proper in trying to rescue me. Probably only the guardian's leniency had saved her from a reprimand, or even punishment.

The officer took me to a Veldqan doctor—I thought at the time—in a third-story office with no evidence of medical facilities. I suspect that social medicine was not stressed in this culture. The strong would survive, while the weak would be allowed to perish under their own inadequacies. The doctor sprinkled a white powder in my wound, bound it, and he was finished. I suspected I would bear a permanent scar on the arm.

Neither the guardian nor the doctor questioned me concerning my supposed amnesia. Apparently they assumed I would recover without medical aid—or not at all. They appeared totally indifferent as to which it would be. No pay was asked or offered.

After the guardian and I left the doctor's office we walked for nearly an hour, until we reached a large barracks-type structure with acres of land surrounding it, resembling an immense meadow, except that it was dotted with smaller buildings that I guessed held military equipment.

The guardian led me to a large room, with perhaps a hundred men sleeping on the high Veldqan pallets. I was directed to one, and the guardian left me. I crawled under the fur covering, without removing anything more than my boots. My arm did not pain yet, and surprisingly I slept soundly.

In the morning another doctor visited me and changed the dressing on my arm while I sat on the edge of my pallet. The arm was sensitive, but not excessively painful. I decided that the medicine they had used was quite effective.

When he finished the doctor said, "Your questioning has been scheduled for this afternoon. You will be summoned at the proper time. Until then you are free to refrain from the exercises."

I had my breakfast standing up. Food, unwarmed, was spread on a long table, and I and the soldiers silently helped ourselves. The main course was a kind of semi-dried meat, and a starchy vegetable resembling a small pumpkin. We washed it down with a bittersweet milk.

After the soldiers finished eating, and cleaning their metal dishes, they formed ranks and marched out to the meadow-like grounds, with me following behind. There they were joined by thousands more, marching from other exits of the building. They quickly separated into detachments and began a series of battle simulations.

Most of the groups broke into individual units, where they fought as though in actual battle, with various types of weapons, swords, pikes, and truncheons predominating.

It took only a few minutes for me to realize that the weapons were blunted, and inflicted no cuts, but there were still a considerable number of casualties. Those struck on the head or other areas vulnerable to the weapons' weight and momentum were hurt, some quite severely.

As an opponent fell the remaining soldier would wait while a team of others—probably their medical corps—carried away the vanquished, and then found another free contestant with whom to continue his fight. I hoped their medical men were experts at concussions and contusions.

These men were being trained and conditioned for actual battle, yet as I had heard it, there was no longer any fighting. There was peace among the clans, and their war preparations could be only a pointless anachronism.

I had little time to speculate on the military activity, for early in the forenoon I received an order to report to the front landing of the barracks.

And there I found Yasi.

"You are now to be free," she said, taking me by an elbow and leading me from the barracks. At my questioning look she nodded her head. "Yes, I am wonderful," she said, in agreement with something she pretended to read in my expression.

"How did you manage it?" I asked.

"It was with such ease," she answered nonchalantly. "I found a proper form, filled in your name, and signed it with my father's name—and presented it to an official in the army department. And that was all of it." She wrinkled her nose, and chuckled in self-congratulation. I smiled also, for there was something of a pixie nature in her that was contagious.

I suspected that she had taken another risk for me, and that in time there might be repercussions, but I was very grateful, and gladly accepted my freedom. "Where are we going now?" I asked.

"To my home," she answered. "They will not think to look for you there."

"You knew then that I had escaped from Trobt?" I asked.

"I did not know, but I had suspected it," she said, very sober. "I was certain you were not one who would die easily."

*   *   *

We walked to Yasi's home, an apartment in one of the stone buildings, as she talked, almost continuously. Without quite realizing it until then, I had developed a deep affection for this small sprightly person.

Once in her apartment Yasi made me strip to the waist, and examined my arm. It had swollen a bit, but there was no sign of infection. "We won't need a . . ." I began, and could come up with no Veldqan word for doctor. The reason? They had none.

"When we are young we are given elementary training in bone setting and the care of wounds," Yasi explained, "and that is all."

The "doctor" the guardian had taken me to then had been only a wound-dresser. That spurning of greater proficiency in medicine fit quite well with what I had already learned of this warrior culture.

After dressing my arm Yasi made me relate everything that had happened to me since she left, in great detail. I detected, however, some impatience, as though she had important affairs of her own to discuss. When finally she was satisfied with my report, she sprang to her feet, and tripped out to the center of the room. "And now for me!" she exclaimed, and began slowly to remove her clothing, laughing merrily all the while. When she finished she did a pirouetting dance about the room, an expectant smile on her face.

I was completely dumbfounded, with no idea what she was up to, or what was expected of me.

"You tease me," Yasi cried, when she saw me sitting with such noncomprehension. She ran slim hands down the sides of her body and across her hips. "Surely you can see?"

I had a moment of acute discomfort. This quick baring of a female body was not something I was accustomed to, and now I did not know how I was to react. This had something to do with Veldqan sexual mores, I was certain, but what? Surely I was not expected to. . . .

Yasi saved me further disconcerting thoughts when she said, "My msst!" throwing the words at me, in simulated anger. "It began only nine days before now."

And at last my perplexity lifted. Msst. The eighth year, when the woman's sterility leaves. I noted the signs of it on

Yasi then, the soft flesh ripening her body, the slight rounding of her hips, and the embryo breasts beginning to push out like small fruit.

"Oh, you are stupid," Yasi taunted my obtuseness, but the softness of her tone belied the words, and she ran to where I sat and climbed like a child into my lap. "You will like me even more when it is complete," she promised, putting both arms around my neck and squeezing mightily. "You will hold me, and hug me, and love me so much," she chatted excitedly. "I will be so wonderful you will not be able to resist me. You will love me so greatly that you will be like a slave to me, but I will be good to you, for I will love you greatly in return. And I will never let you go away," she finished, only because she was out of breath.

Veldqan impetuousness is not confined to the males, I told myself, as I sat holding the girl-child in my arms, not quite knowing what to do or say.

Yasi, however, was oblivious to my embarrassment, content to furnish all the conversation. "I marked you at the highest summit," she said, looking at me coquettishly through her long lashes. And again I was without comprehension.

"You—big—big—stupid," she crooned, punctuating each word with a kiss on my cheek. She drew back her head, obviously very happy and contented. "I should not be telling you our woman secrets," she said, "but we women all observe you foolish men during our long still period, and when we are ready, we have made our choice." She smiled brightly. "You think that it is you men who make the choice of us, but you are powerless to resist us then, and we are the ones who decide who will love us."

Her mood changed abruptly and she buried her face against my neck and I could feel its dampness. "I was afraid you would not live till then." She shifted position in my arms, which, unaware, I had put around her. "But you are alive, alive, alive." She kissed me three times, quickly, hungrily, on the lips.

I wonder if any man could have reacted other than humbly before the lightning vagaries of Yasi's moods. Apparently the woman's transformation period is one of high emotional fluctuation. The only self-assertion I could present was to follow my instinct. I took her sweet child's face in both my hands and kissed her again, very tenderly.

I stayed with Yasi for seven days, and each day brought further small delightful advances in her womanhood. The complete process would involve approximately twenty days, she told me.

I did not let her mercurial, absorbing presence keep me from my work. Each day I went out, going on with my investigation. My view of the Veldqans as being brutal, violent, and merciless was often confirmed. I watched men fight over some fancied insult, or some woman in her msst, who was no more than casually interested in either of the contestants, or for no more than simple enjoyment, and over their rigid mores that were no longer functional, and I despised them.

Their admiration of pointless courage saddened me with its emptiness whenever I was forced to witness it. They engaged in games of conflict—not confined to the military—with no ill-will on either side, merely for the thrill and pseudo-Honor of victory—that often left one or the other participant maimed or crippled. They fought because of their need to share exhilarating conflict. They were the spawn of generations of fighters who, with the passing of the dleeth, and the union of the tribes, had no one to fight except each other.

I detected also what might have been a universal discontent in their young men. They had a warrior heritage and nature which, with the unity of the tribes, left them with an unrealized futility of purpose. And the custom of polygamy—functional in the old days, and pursued still by those able to attain it—left the unfortunate ones sexually frustrated. I saw that they did not even know the reason for their discontent, let alone what its solution might be.

They had not quite been able to achieve a successful sublimation of their post-warrior need to fight in the Games. It was not enough—the biological needs of their natures were too powerful—and the Games served only as temporary stopgaps. Their male frustration was potentially explosive.

Gradually, however, the picture I had of them in my mind altered. As new facts and understanding entered, the lines and pattern shifted and the picture changed. The murky whole had begun to reveal patches of light, shadows faded into the background, and other shadows showed the gray of sadness, where before there had been only the black of ugliness.

The first realization I had of the change in the picture came when I became satisfied that Veldq had no crime; other than in rare individual instances, lying, theft, and deceit were practically unknown. And this because of fineness of racial character rather than because of effective restraint.

With the near completion of the picture my dislike for them changed to admiration—tempered by touches of pity and sorrow. Pity when I saw their dissatisfaction, their discontent with their lives, and their inability to combat it.

And, weighing what I observed of the tide that carried them, I decided that I liked them. The manners and organization of the Veldqans—within the framework of their culture—were as simple and effective as their architecture. There was a strong emphasis on pride, on strength and honor, on skill, and on living a dangerous life with a gambler's self-command, on rectitude, on truth, and the unbreakable bond of loyalty to family and friends. All this I saw and admired.

I weighed all this when I reacted to the Veldqans, and toward the end a strange feeling—a kind of wistfulness—came as I observed them. I felt kin to them, as if these people had much in common with myself. And I felt that it was too bad that life was not fundamentally so simple that one could discard the awareness of other ways of life, of other competing values and philosophies, and made one doubt his own philosophy. Too bad that I could not see and take life that directly, and that simply.

The last day of my stay with Yasi I returned at last to the power station, and this time I examined it thoroughly, both above and below ground. I found no cables, and no way to enter. I might have realized the small possibility of finding anything there. There were no waterfalls or swift current to supply power, and no evidence of a fuel being consumed. The station was at best a transmitter.

I climbed a spiral ramp that went around the outside of the station until I reached the top. My thought was that I might be able to see other cities in the distance, or evidence of agriculture, or even points of interest within Hearth that I had missed.

The top of the tower, I found, was concave, with a four-bladed propeller—parallel to the roof—turning slowly on a spindly rod at its center. The impression I received was of a huge ornamental windmill lying on its side. I had no idea what its purpose might be.

I sat on the top of a wide railing at the edge of the roof and gazed out over the wall of the city. There was no evidence of agriculture. On all sides—as far as I could see—was nothing but red sand. Trackless red sand, making small whirlpools in the cold wind, and coming right up to the walls of the city.

On all sides except one. To my left, stretching out from Hearth until lost in the distance, was a long twin ribbon of concrete road. And on the road were dozens of slowly crawling vehicles that might have been Caterpillar trucks of Earth.

In my mind the pattern clicked into place. Hearth was not typical of the cities of Veldq!

It was an anachronism, a revered Homeplace, a symbol of the past, untainted by the technology that was pursued elsewhere. This was the capital city, from which the heads of government still ruled, perhaps for sentimental reasons, but it was not typical. That also was why I had seen so little evidence of advanced implements and machinery in Hearth. I sprang to my feet and began pacing the narrow roof, lost in contemplation.

One of the enigmas of this civilization, I pondered, had been lurking just beneath the surface of my brain, and now came out and took concrete form: how was it possible for a race still in its nomad stage to have a high technology—at least in its weapons development?

Civilizations, as I understood them, passed through three stages—nomad, pastoral, and technological. In the nomad stage tribes subsisted on their natural resources, animals, grains, and fruits. Usually they followed the herds of their principal meat sources, as the Earth Eskimos followed the caribou, and the Indians the buffalo. Later they domesticated animals and directed their migrations from region to region, as the animals' food needs dictated.

They moved from that to the pastoral stage when they learned to grow crops, both for themselves and their animals. Their wanderings ceased then, and subtle changes took place in their society, and in their life-styles. Gradually their aggressiveness left them, and they learned to live more disciplined lives. They became more *pastoral*.

In time some members grew skilled in individual trades, as in cloth and garment making, the fashioning of tools and agricultural implements, and they met in central locations to sell their wares. Those central places grew larger, and in time became cities, and the trades gradually became automated, and more sophisticated—and they were in the technology stage.

Veldq seemed to have jumped from the nomad period directly into the technological. Which I had always believed impossible. Without the introduction of outside help. Was there an answer in that? No answer came from the annotator.

All the evidence I had unearthed in Hearth—though that must comprise no more than one or two percent of the planet's population—indicated that it was still in the nomad stage. Yet the evidence of the spaceships and superior weapons, as well as the transportation vehicles I saw here, meant its citizens had to have a higher technology.

7

Now I knew I was done with caution. There was little more to be learned in Hearth; I would go out and learn what I could of the apparent anomaly of a high technical development in a nomad society, find their factories, and learn what I could. . . .

The decision to be made now was how I would travel. I could take a tricar and set out along the highway until I reached a factory city, but the weakness in that plan was that I was uncertain of the range of the small cars; mine might never get me to my destination.

An alert from the annotator sounded, and I sat down again on the station's wide railing and began recording on my twitch tape everything that had happened lately that might be of value—including on the roads outside.

Afterward I climbed down the outside stairway, and set out for the nearest gate in the city wall.

I had a vague sense of eager anticipation as I went out and trudged across the red sands toward the slowly moving flat trucks. One of the last remaining puzzles here should be solved within a relatively short time, I was convinced.

The trucks, I had observed from the wall, were driverless,

and as I neared them I saw that they were held to the roads by magnetic metal stripes running down the middles.

The cars going to my right carried metal machinery parts, those going to the left complete units, many of them large. I caught a truck going to the right. I wanted to see the factories where the parts were assembled.

The "red giant" sun came out from behind the clouds as I began my ride, raising the early fall temperature into the low seventies. There was no wind, and no sign of precipitation. It was a superlatively fine day, and augured well for the success of my journey.

I stripped to the waist, and let the hot sun have its way with my skin, and bring healing warmth to every cell in my body— as it felt. The accumulated tensions left my muscles, and I stretched out on the truck platform with a complete lack of concern for all that had harried me the past several weeks.

I must have dozed, for I opened my eyes to find that we had left the red sands and were riding through grassland that stretched for miles on both sides. In the distance ahead a low mountain bulked large against the skyline. The sun had disappeared behind the clouds again, and the temperature had dropped considerably. I put on my leather blouse, but not my cloak.

Awhile later I left the truck and trotted beside it, getting the exercise I had to have on this alien world. When I returned to my platform I noticed that my boots were covered with a fine white dust. I brushed them off, and sat watching the surrounding landscape go by.

As we neared the mountain and entered a long range of foothills I could see the smoke of a brush fire spreading out over a growth of low trees. I could not see the fire, but soon caught its aromatic scent.

As though ordered, rain began to fall, in a slow steady drizzle. I put on my cloak and huddled against the nearest machinery crate. The rain was warm, however, and I was not too uncomfortable.

Abruptly the day grew darker, and the sky seemed to explode in a succession of sound and light flashes, and the rain became a cloudburst. Soon the surface of the mountain began oozing white blood that worked its way out through the vine capillaries and down the hillsides, flooding the plain on which our tracks were set. The trucks, however, never paused.

I realized that the white of the streamlets coming down the mountainside was limestone, which must form the bulk of the mountain. I remember reading a paper, "On a Piece of Chalk," by an ancient English writer named Thomas Huxley, and I recognized what I was seeing, as snatches of the article rose from my memory banks:

> Calcareous skeletons formed by minute living creatures. . . . Substance too soft to be called rock . . . familiar chalk. . . . Where the thin soils that covered it had washed away. . . . Attaining a thickness of more than a thousand feet. (Extending out from Harwich) it forms an irregular oval about three thousand miles in diameter. . . . underlies Paris . . . through Denmark and Central Europe and southward to North Africa . . . Crimea and in Syria . . . to the shores of the Sea of Aral.

That explained also the white dust that had gathered on my boots as I walked.

The rain stopped as gradually as it had begun, and the sun returned reluctantly, as the truck train continued on its way.

Only as the sun began to set did I see signs of Veldqans, a small town by the side of the road. None of the inhabitants were near enough to notice me riding the truck.

I debated leaving the vehicle and going into the town, but decided against it; the place was too small to be an important manufacturing center.

However, a short while later, I felt the truck take a slight dip—and I was underground. In a huge factory!

On all sides silent machines spewed out metal machinery parts, which were deposited on belts and conveyed to other sections of the underground. To be assembled, it was not difficult to surmise.

All the machines were completely automated. This might

have been a manufacturing complex on any of the Ten Thousand Worlds.

The place must have a central observation post, but I saw no evidence of overseers, and no one bothered me. I rode deeper into the underground, noting other long tunnels branching off from the main artery in which I rode. If they had other factories this large, in other locations—which I questioned—the output would be enormous.

I rode deeper into the complex, gradually nearing the source of an all-pervasive hum, until I came to a room that housed a squat, potbellied boiler. The source of the hum.

It could be nothing other than a Balscon burner!

Inside the machine, if I was right, lithium was being subjected to laser-ray bombardment, and ignited, to provide a vast amount of energy. The power generated there could easily run the entire factory, with a considerable amount left over. And a still unformed supposition began to take shape in my mind.

I jumped from the carrier and hurried over to the potbellied machine, where my suspicions were confirmed. On the machine's side was printed: Minnesota Mining and Manufacturing Company, St Paul, Minnesota.

And this portion of the puzzle of Veldq was solved. All this technology had been borrowed, or stolen, from the Ten Thousand Worlds!

And we were being challenged by this sparsely populated planet, without even a technology of its own. On the face of it that was absurd. However. . . . That devastating weapon. . . .

This at least solved the problem of the missing pastoral stage.

I walked from the underground then, and made my way into the small settlement bordering the installations. This was the home of the supervisors, engineers, and maintenance workers—and their families, probably—I surmised.

I verified that fact while I ate in one of their public restaurants. I would not be seeking a place to sleep, I had decided, for I would return to Hearth as soon as I finished eating. I had learned all I would here.

I had spotted a table and an empty couch in the rear of the

eating place, and worked my way toward it, having to ignore the hopeful glance of a lounger, wanting a Game, I suspected.

I had not eaten for nearly twelve hours, and I had a substantial meal, and afterward sat contentedly, a bit drowsy. Mainly the drowsiness was caused by my long time without sleep, and the meal, but, also, I was feeling a considerable satisfaction with what I had learned here, and I was as relaxed as I'd been in a long while.

Many of the customers in the place were not diners, I noticed as I sat back contentedly, but drank a colored liquid from clear glass tumblers. Alcohol of some kind, I guessed. I decided to try some.

I put in my order, was served, and tried a tentative swallow. The liquor burned a path across my tongue and down my throat, bringing tears to my eyes. It was definitely not as mild as it appeared. The second swallow went down somewhat easier.

The voices around me had quieted while I tasted my drink, and I looked up apprehensively, but everyone's attention was directed toward the front of the room. All about them was an air of expectancy, and a latent excitement. Abruptly then the room became eerily still, the spectators motionless, and I followed their gaze to the front entrance.

To where a woman stood with a casual indolence.

She was a woman of breathtaking presence, dressed all in white, standing cool and poised, very sure of herself. Her body had none of the sterile bleakness of the boy-girls, but was rounded firmly, slim at the waist and swelling ripely above and below, full-fleshed and sensuous. As she walked then across the room a thin slit running down the length of her blouse alternately parted and closed, exposing a narrow section of breasts and diaphragm. It was a quite stimulating revelation.

This, it developed, was the spectator's entertainment, their floor show, except that the woman did not dance or act, she merely walked—which was obviously entertainment enough. Every man in the room, myself included, followed her casual moves with rapt fascination, and once when her glance paused on mine I became suddenly shy and awkward—and excited. I was glad when she turned away, for I was certain that otherwise my closely contained reserve would have broken, and I would have done something callow.

She came down the center aisle then, and as she neared me I caught a sweet delicate scent of musk, that instinctively I knew came from the very pores of the flesh itself. I was affected much as the male moth who can detect a female's scent for miles and is inexorably drawn to it.

On Earth certain rather prissy mores forbid mention of the part the female scent plays in sexual stimulation, though everyone knows of it. Here it was not cloaked behind pseudo-gentility. The woman's eighth year, her fertility period, is called her msst, from the name of the scent she exudes. It is not something of which she is ashamed, but the sign of her rampant readiness to mate, the signal to the males that nature has prepared her for her role in the propagation of the race. With the Veldqan women's limited birthrate, nature made certain that when she was ready the male would never be reluctant to perform his role.

Now that I was exposed to the msst for the first time, a slow pulse began to throb quickly in my throat, a rush of stimulation came up from deep within, and an abrupt hunger grew in my tissues. With amazement I realized that this was the biological response of my glands to her mere presence. And her scent. I reached out blindly for my goblet and drained it.

I left the eating and drinking place soon after—and made my way to the flatcars. I boarded one going back the way I had come.

I slept most of the night, awakening only when some inner caution alerted me that I had reached Hearth. I alighted and trudged through the red sand toward the nearest gate in the walls, and went in.

Trobt was waiting for me inside.

I was resigned to seeing Trobt, more or less expecting it, and offered no resistance, or objections when he asked, in his always polite way, "Will you come with me, please?"

He made no motion to go, however, and when I looked into his face I saw that he shared the same unease. I had the certainty that if either of us had given the slightest gesture of acceptance, we would have embraced each other. And the reflex action would have been extremely distasteful to us both.

As I might have expected, Trobt showed no sign of anger with me for having evaded his guards and fleeing to the City. His was the universal Veldqan viewpoint. To them all life was the Game—with the difference that it is played on an infinitely larger Board. Every man and every woman with whom the player had contact, direct or indirect, were pukts on the Board. The player made his decisions, and his plays, and how well he made them determined whether he won or lost. His every move, his every joining of strength with those who would help him, his every maneuver against those who opposed him, was his choice to make, and he rose or fell on the wisdom of his choice. Game, in Veldqan, means Duel, means struggle and the test of man against the opponent, Life. I had made my escape as the best play as I saw it. Trobt would have no recriminations.

That evening Trobt and I discussed my trip to the underground factory. "You know by now that we borrowed most of our technology from your Ten Thousand Worlds, I presume?" he introduced.

I nodded, pleased that he had brought up the subject. "Why did you conceal it?" I asked.

He considered that. "Pride, I suppose, is my only excuse," he answered. "I didn't want you to know that we hadn't advanced as far as you thought."

"How were you able to acquire all that machinery?" I questioned.

"By the simple process of buying it," he replied. "In much the same way one of your Worlds buys from another."

For some reason Trobt was being evasive, giving answers but explaining little. Was his pride still restraining him? "It doesn't seem it would be that simple," I objected. "You would need a large organization, and you had to keep your identity a secret."

"A point you may be missing—" Trobt began again, "You have to understand that that purchasing has been going on for well over a half-century. We do have a quite large organization, but nearly all of it is stationed right here on Veldq."

"You discovered us that long ago?" My curiosity led me to digress.

"That shouldn't be too surprising," Trobt replied. "Our world is a grain of sand among a billion, while you, with your numbers, your many settlements and ships of trade, would not be likely to escape our notice."

"Will you give me more details on how you made your purchases?" I returned to my main topic of interest.

Trobt sighed. "I see you will be satisfied with nothing less than a complete explanation," he said good-naturedly. "Over a period of time we established a network of depots on outlying asteroids. We'd order by spacegram and have our goods delivered to the depots. There was no reason for them to suspect that the orders were not from other Worlds. Actually it all went quite smoothly. In fact, it still does."

"You pay for the goods with raw materials, I would guess?" I saw how an intelligent, efficient organization would make the task less difficult than I had at first supposed.

"We bring the raw materials to the asteroid depots. Your ships deliver one and pick up the other. It is seldom necessary for them even to see one of us. Though when that is necessary, it makes small difference."

So much for that.

"I perceive that this is more than simple personal curiosity," Trobt was not finished yet. "It's impossible for you to escape, and you must realize that. Yet you persist in your quest for information." He smiled slightly. "Do you have some means of communication with your Worlds?"

I hoped my incredulous laugh was convincing.

I had a few questions remaining—if Trobt would still answer them.

"You had to have space flight before the activities you mentioned would have been possible," I pointed out. "Will you tell me how you discovered that?"

"The answer should be obvious," Trobt teased me.

"A prodigy developed it?" I guessed.

"Hardly likely. The answer is even more simple. One of your spaceships crashed on Veldq—and though disabled, was not damaged badly."

Of course.

"We gave top priority to studying that ship, and repairing. it," Trobt said. "In time we learned just about all it had to give us."

"It still seems like an impossible task, with your small knowledge of technology," I protested.

"It took us eighty-seven years before we were even able to fly the ship."

With perseverance like that much is possible.

"You said you have a weapon that destroyed our fleet?" My final question. "A prodigy this time?" I thought to add.

"No. In studying your spaceship, after it crashed, we experimented—". He halted abruptly, and shook his head when I made to question him further. "That will be all of that," he said. "You will have to be satisfied with what I've already told you."

He had made a slip there. Our own weapons, then, probably needed only an adjustment. . . .

I began recording on the twitch tape immediately.

Thus far we had not discussed the coming Final Game. I was prepared, mentally, to meet it anytime, but Trobt's attitude seemed to indicate that it had been postponed indefinitely. Why, I could not tell. As usual, I retired early that night.

The following evening Trobt returned from his office earlier than usual. We had a leisurely meal, and afterward sat for a time, chatting idly. When sometime later he asked, "Would you care to play a Game?" I readily agreed, but something about the tone of his words suggested that there was more to the request than I had caught, and I waited for what was to follow.

"This will be the most difficult game you've ever played— Game or chess," Trobt said—confirming my suspicion—and walked to the place where our cloaks hung, and took down both his and mine. "The wind is chilly this evening," he said, and I wondered at his air of mystery. And triumph, as though he were about to prove something to me, something that I had disputed earlier.

We put on our cloaks and I followed Trobt out to the tricar ramp, still without knowing where we were going. He drove diagonally away from the River Widd, but our journey was not long, for Hearth is quite narrow and we approached the city wall after only a short drive.

The territory we stopped in was old and poorly lighted, as near to an Earth slum as I had seen here, and obviously one of the original sections of Hearth. Many of the houses were abandoned, and most of the others were in poor repair.

We parked our tricar on a side avenue and walked perhaps a hundred yards. Trobt seemed strangely subdued by this time, as though ashamed of something he was about to reveal, but he said nothing.

"If you win this Game perhaps I will have to change my opinion of Humans," Trobt said, partly in jest, seeming to want to lighten his solemnity. Whatever was about to happen here, I thought, it might be an opportunity to do a positive service for my side. I hoped my confidence would prove justified.

We stopped at the door of a small one-story stone house and Trobt tapped with his fingernails on a gong buried in a hollow in the wood.

After a minute a curtain over the door glass was drawn back and an old woman with straggly gray hair peered out at us. She recognized Trobt and opened the door. We went in.

The hut had only one room, with packed earth the only floor, and was furnished with sturdy furniture, built to last a lifetime and more. A fireplace burned low at one end of the room, heating it just to the edge of comfort, and from the farthest corner a doglike animal stared at us with baleful yellow eyes.

The old woman did not speak to Trobt, but turned her back to us, and went to stir embers in the stone grate. She wore a blanket-dress, and thick-soled shoes, to protect her from the room's chill and the floor's even rawer cold.

Trobt gave no evidence of being aware of the woman's deliberate inhospitality, and motioned with his head for me to follow, and led the way to a bed at the left side of the room.

"Leonard Stromberg," he said, "I would like you to meet Yondtl."

I looked to the bed, where Trobt had indicated. My first

impression was of a great white blob, propped up on the bed and supported by the wall at its back.

Then the thing moved—moved its eyes—and I knew that it was alive. Its eyes told me also that it was a man. If I could call it a man.

The head was large and bloated, with blue eyes washed almost colorless, peering out from deep pouches of flesh. He seemed to have no neck, almost as though his great head were merely an extension of the trunk, separated only by puffy folds of fat. Other lappings of flesh hung from his body in great thick rolls.

It took another minute of absorbed inspection before I saw that he had no arms, and that no legs reached from his body to the floor. The entire sight of him made me want to leave the room and be sick.

"Leonard Stromberg is an Earthian who would challenge you, sir," Trobt addressed the monstrosity.

The other gave no sign that I could see but Trobt went to the far side of the bed and pulled a game table over to us. "I will serve as his hands," Trobt said.

The pale blue eyes never left my face.

I stood without conscious thought until Trobt pushed a chair under me. Mentally I shook myself. With unsteady hands—I had to do something with them—I reached for the pukts before me. "Do you…do you have a choice…of colors, sir?" I stammered, trying to make up for my earlier staring.

The lips of the monstrosity quivered, but no sound came.

All the while Trobt had been watching me with amusement. "He is deaf and speechless," Trobt said. "Take either set. He will use the other."

Absentmindedly I pulled the red pieces toward me and placed them on their squares.

In deference to you as a visitor, you will play 'second game counts,'" Trobt told me. He was still enjoying my consternation. "He always allows his opponent the first move. You may begin when you are ready."

With an effort I forced myself to concentrate on the playing board. My start, I decided, must be orthodox. I had to learn something of the type of game this—Yondtl—played. I moved my first-row pukt its two oblique and one left squares.

Yondtl inclined his head slightly. His lips moved. Trobt put his hand on a pukt and pushed it forward. Evidently Trobt read his lips. Very probably Yondtl could read ours also.

I tried several gambits that invited a mistake on Yondtl's part. He made none. When he offered I was careful to make no mistake of my own. We both played as though this first game were the whole contest.

An hour passed. I had deliberately traded three pukts with Yondtl in an attempt to trick him into a misplay. None came.

I tried a single decoy gambit, and when nothing happened, followed with a second decoy. Yondtl countered each play. I marveled that he gave so little of his attention to the board. Always he seemed to be watching me. I played. He played. He watched me.

I perspired.

Yondtl set up an overt pass that forced me to draw my pukts back into the main body. Somehow I received the impression that he was teasing me. It made me more determined to beat him.

I decided on a crossed-force double gambit. I had never seen it employed. Because, I suspect, it is too involved, and open to error by its user. Slowly and painstakingly I set it up and pressed forward.

The Caliban in the seat opposite me never paused. He matched me play for play. And though his features had long since lost the power of expression, his pale eyes seemed to develop a blue luster. I realized, almost with a shock of surprise, that that gross caricature of a man was happy—intensely happy.

I came out of my reverie with a start. Yondtl had made an obvious play, I an obvious counter. I was startled to hear him sound a cry that might have been a muffled shout, or an idiot's laugh, and my attention jerked back to the board.

I had lost the game!

My brief moment of abstraction had given Yondtl the opportunity to make a pass too subtle to be detected with part of my faculties occupied elsewhere.

The Game was not actually over, I continued to do my

best, hoping to regain equity, to force him into a similar mis-play, but knew that my one mistake had been fatal, and after a half hour, when I could make no gain, I surrendered as gracefully as possible. Discovering only then that I was not a particularly good loser.

We began the second game—and still I hadn't found a weakness in my opponent. Worse, I had learned that any slight lapse of attention on my own part would be fatal.

Now I had to play a faultless game, while still searching for Yondtl's weak point. The obvious course, I decided, would be to try a play of elimination. I had used it often before to find an opponent's weakness. I could play it in such a way as to be almost certain not to make a mistake. The worst I could get would be a standoff. And perhaps Yondtl could not play as perfect a game with fewer pieces. I would find out.

Slowly, carefully, I moved my pukts, taking every opportunity for a safe exchange. After each play, and particularly after each exchange, I looked for signs of error, or at least uncertainty, in Yondtl's play. I found none. With each lessening of pukts I tried new gambits. Always Yondtl matched them.

The game ended when we each had one pukt remaining. It was no game. I tried to console myself by the fact that I had done better than in the first game. The next I should win. I didn't entirely convince myself.

For some time I had been watching for a sign of weariness in Yondtl—in his poor physical condition he should not have too much stamina—but when I glanced at him I saw that the glisten of happiness in his eyes burned unabated. And conversely, I was near exhaustion. This was the most severe mental stress I had ever experienced. In this condition, I'd be a fool to try him again, I decided.

I pushed back my chair. "That will be enough for tonight," I told Trobt. If I were to do the Human race a service I needed rest before trying Yondtl again.

We made arrangements to meet the following evening—and seeing that the old woman was dozing in a chair by the fireplace—we let ourselves out.

On the drive back it was I who was silent. I had a fairly

definite presentiment that I had met my match—and probably
more.

When we reached Trobt's home he left me for a minute
and came back with a flagon of liquor and two goblets. He
filled both and gave one to me. I held my glass wonderingly
as he raised his in a silent toast, then drained it. He was as
near to showing exhilaration as I'd ever seen him.

"Tonight," he said, speaking Earthian, "I feel a need to talk.
Will you bear with me?"

I smiled my agreement.

"Why am I happy?" he asked. "Because you have met a
Veldqan you cannot beat," he answered his own question.
"Always before there was this small doubt in my mind. Here,
I said, is this Human, whipping us at our own Game. True,
he may be the best of the Humans. But he is beating the best
of the Veldqans. Are the Humans then more intelligent? Tonight it was answered. Our best is better than your best!"

He raised his hand to stop me when he thought I would
speak. "Oh, I know. You have not lost yet. But you will.
Yondtl will beat you!"

It was not a subject I cared to debate. "What is Yondtl?"
I asked. "An idiot savant?"

Trobt shook his head. "He is the most intelligent man of
Veldq. "He would hold my position, except—" He spread his
hands wide. "Well, you saw him."

"How does it happen that he still lives?" I asked. "If I understand your mores, he should have been smothered in his
cradle."

Trobt was on his feet by the time I'd finished speaking.
However, he seemed to change his mind in mid-rising, and
poured himself a second goblet of liquor. He did not pour one
for me.

He was more sober then, and I could tell by his short clipped
speech that he was feeling some emotion that would have been
anger against anyone else. But we had by this time arrived at
such an understanding of each other that true anger was un-
likely. He relaxed then, and belatedly filled my glass.

"Do you remember when I stopped in the park with you
and explained why you would die?" he asked. "That was very

unusual, for me or any other Veldqan. If you recall I spoke low. I did not want the others to hear me. They would not have understood." His sentences still came out sharp and direct. "On Veldq it is an insult to ask a man his reasons. He does what he believes right. He will never explain his actions. If you question them you are impugning his Honor. I did something very disagreeable for me when I explained my actions to you. I wanted you to see us as we are, not to think us savages. What you ask me now is that kind of insult."

This was a part of the Veldqan nature I still did not understand. "But why?" I asked. "It was a matter of mere curiosity. You know I meant no offense. Why should you be angry?"

"What you say is true, in your way to think of it." He hesitated. "What is your word for it? Indelicate! That is it. Except in a much stronger sense."

He saw that the explanation meant little to me. "Wait. One minute," he said. "I understand your ways even less than you do ours, but I should be able to find some situation on your Worlds to demonstrate what I mean."

"Here," he resumed after a minute. "You visit a friend when he returns from his first marriage journey. Perhaps there are other friends present. You are introduced to his mate, and admire her beauty. You ask him, 'And did you find her a virgin?'

"You mean no harm. You are not being unduly curious. You are certain that he did find her such, and will be happy to reveal it." He paused. "Do you see the indelicacy of it, the insult, even though he may recognize your good intentions?"

"Of course," I answered contritely.

"Are you surprised then," Trobt went on, "when he does not tell you, joyfully, that she was indeed a virgin? Or that he does not explain, that while she had not been a virgin, there had been only two others whereas the average. . . ."

The laughter I could not hold back halted him. He looked up in surprise. Even when I realized that he wasn't jesting, by his nature couldn't be, I was unable to stop. "I am convinced, I am convinced," I finally managed to answer.

"Now." Truly Trobt felt like talking that night. "You ask why Yondtl still lives. I will repress my indignation and tell you. Yondtl is my shame. Others also—but mine more. And I do not know how to erase that shame.

"You are correct in believing that he should have been destroyed at birth. But his mother loved him too much. She hid him and we never heard of his conception. For years she fed and cared for him, and kept her secret.

"As Yondtl grew older his need for intellectual stimulation led him to make a few friends, with whom he conversed and played the Game. The circle of those who knew him grew as his genius evidenced itself. Eventually the knowledge reached the Council.

"I went with several guardians to take him to a place of painless sleep. It is a very disagreeable task—putting to death a man who can look into your eyes and beg with his gaze to know why this is being done—more difficult than destroying a baby who has not yet reached the age of reason.

"Still, I could not permit that to keep me from my duty, and I did not shirk it. But his mother—" Trobt's expression revealed that the recollection was still painful. "When I arrived, and the guardians made ready to carry Yondtl out, his old mother—you saw her—fell to her knees and clutched my cloak, begging me not to take her son.

"Can you picture it?" Trobt was visibly moved. "That old woman, on her knees, groveling at my feet, kissing my boots, deliberately debasing herself, weeping and begging me to spare her son.

"The embarrassment of it, the humiliation I felt because of what I was forced to watch her do. Can you imagine my emotions, my shame? What was I to do? Could I push that miserable wretch aside, tear her hands from my cloak, and carry the only thing she loved from her house?

"I ran, actually ran, out into the street." When he finished Trobt sat with head bent.

"You did right," I said softly.

"Right?" He was indignant. "Could I let him live, and not be forced in conscience to allow every miserable misfit on Veldq to live also? In a few generations the strength of our clansmen would be dissipated by my folly. I would be Veldq's most despicable traitor. Which I am!"

I reached to touch his shoulder, but he jerked away and

strode from the room. There would be no more talking that night.

This time I understood him. Completely. Yondtl was Trobt's scarlet letter.

I did not follow Trobt's example and go directly to bed. Instead I filled my rock tub to the rim and let myself luxuriate in its steamy comfort. Gradually the sense of well-being I had experienced on the truck train returned, and I was content. I made no effort to consider my upcoming Game with Yondtl; that night was for restoration, the next day I would think. Afterward I went to bed and slept the sleep of *fidus Achates.*

I awoke at daybreak, with all my senses alert. I had much thinking to do before evening came. Trobt had told me on the ride back the night before, that to the best of his knowledge, Yondtl had never lost a Game. Which only confirmed my earlier conviction that our next meeting would be the ultimate test of my ability. I would have to plan my stratagems as fully and as well as I was able before we met again. And those stratagems must be excellent. Anything less than my very best would not be enough.

I considered first what Yondtl's weaknesses might be. It has always been my conviction that every man has at least one. In my mind I reviewed all our play, reenacting the gambits he had used, mine, and the means he had employed to evade them. I tried to find moves he had made that might have been better executed. My eventual conclusion was that if he had a weakness, he had not yet revealed it. I was almost ready to believe that he had none.

Next I made a balance sheet in my mind and weighed our assets.

For Yondtl I put down a brilliant mind, cold logic, innate power of concentration, mental stamina, and faultless execution. A formidable array.

On my side I conceded equal logic and adeptness of execution. I had, in addition to my gift of perception—my ability to spot an opponent's weakness—perhaps to a greater degree than Yondtl could. But of what aid would it be to me against a player who gave no evidence of ever making a mistake?

Finally, though Yondtl had shown no weakness, I had! As

this was not my first knowledge of it I was able to see the fault very plainly. My mind was too inquisitive, too eager to learn all it could about everything it saw, for the kind of competition in which I now had to engage. In the Game it robbed me of just a fraction of the concentration I needed when I played Yondtl. There was the small consolation that having recognized the weakness I would be doubly careful to guard against it.

Also, there was the annotator. Its inquisitiveness might spoil my concentration if I allowed it, but to balance that, it should be my greatest strength. It had seldom failed me in the past.

In addition, I felt keenly alert. My reflexes were primed, sharp and ready for the coming encounter. Having given the problem my best, I was satisfied. I ate my midafternoon meal and lay on my pallet and slept. Soundly, which meant that my subconscious was content with my summations. I would give a good account of myself.

There was no conversation between Trobt and me as we rode to Yondtl's house, and none after we entered. I sat opposite Yondtl, and Trobt brought over the play board. Again I chose the red.

And the Game began.

At the start I discovered that I had made one other decision. Playing the way I had I would never beat Yondtl, a standoff was the best I could hope for. The time had come, therefore, for more consummate action. I would engage him in a triple decoy gambit!

I had no illusion that I could handle it—in the manner it should be handled. I doubt that any man, Human or Veldqan, could. But at least I would play it with the greatest skill I had, giving my best to every move, and push up the scale of reasoning and involution—on and up—until either Yondtl or I became lost in its innumerable complexities, and fell.

As I attacked, the complexes and complications would gradually grow more numerous, become more and more difficult, until they embraced a span greater than one or the other of us had the capacity to encompass, and the other would win.

The Game began and I forced it into the pattern I had planned. Each play, and each maneuver, became all-impor-

tant, demanding the greatest skill I could command. Each
pulled at the core of my brain, dragging out the last iota of
sentient stuff that writhed there.

Yondtl stayed with me, complex gambit through complex
gambit.

When the strain became too great I forced my mind to
pause, to rest, and to be ready for the next clash. I was careful
not to let the unwavering stare of those bleached-blue eyes
disconcert me when they met mine.

At the first break I searched the annotator. It was working
steadily, with an almost smooth throb of efficiency, keeping
the position of each pukt, and its value, strong in the forefront
of visualization.

But something was missing!

A minute went by before I spotted the fault. The move of
each pukt involved so many possibilities, so many avenues of
choice, that no exact answer was predictable on any one. The
number and variation of gambits open on every play, each
subject to the multitude of Yondtl's counter-moves, stretched
the possibilities beyond prediction. The annotator was a har-
monizing, perceptive force, but not a creative, initiating one.

It resembled an Earth computer, given the problem of the
time a spaceship would need to travel from one planet to
another. It had the weight, volume, and fuel potentialities of
the vessel, the drag of the planets' gravities, the course, and
all other relevant factors, everything it needed. Except the
distance between the planets.

The annotator, and the computer, operated in a statistical
manner, and could not perform effectively where a crucial
factor or factors were unknown, or concealed, as they were
here.

My greatest asset had been negated.

Hour after hour the contest went on, with both of us giving
our most minute attention to the play board. Yondtl no longer
kept his rapt gaze on my face, but concentrated all his mental
resources on the board.

At the end of the third hour I began to feel a steady pain
in my temples, as though a tight metal band pressed against
my forehead and squeezed it inward. I rested, and searched

Yondtl's face for any reaction I might be able to use. The only response I discerned was that the blue glint in his eyes had grown brighter. All his happiness was gathered there.

At the end of the fifth hour my pauses became more frequent. Great waves of brain weariness had to be allowed to subside before I could play again.

And at last it came.

Suddenly, unexpectedly, Yondtl had a pukt thrown across the board and took my second decoy, a key weapon—and there was no way for me to retaliate. I had tried all my evasions and tricks on him before, and knew them to be in vain. I could never defeat him once he gained an advantage.

I felt a kind of calm dismay. My shoulders sagged and I pushed the board away from me and slumped in my chair.

I had been beaten.

8

The next two days were very quiet. Trobt made no effort to seek me out—I presume in deference to how he knew I must feel. I had my meals in my room, and skipped my evening walks. I suppose it could have been said that I was sulking. But I had good reason. Not only had I lost to Yondtl, but I had a feel of drowning, of becoming ever more entangled in the mesh of the trap into which I had gotten myself. I had been able to do nothing to help the Ten Thousand Worlds, and my own crisis had but one predictable end.

Predictable because by now I understood fairly well the nature of the culture that had ensnared me. This warrior nation had warrior ethics. They would pass on to their captives and enemies the strain most familiar to them, the endurance test. The test where a man is expected to go to his breaking point, and beyond. I had not even the consolation that I would refuse to fight that long. I knew that I would—for myself, and for the pride of the race from which I had sprung. Those two days were dreary.

The evening of the second day Trobt woke me. I had heard him moving about the house during the day, and knew that he had not gone to the office in the morning as he usually did. I saw then that he too had spent a long day. His face was pale, and his eyes circled, as though smeared with gray ash. His body too was somewhat strained, as though it was only then relaxing from a long ordeal.

All of which was extremely ominous. My instincts told me that I was the cause of his discomfort, that he was forcing himself to do a duty that was distasteful to him—but which he would not try to evade.

He sat on the edge of my pallet, not waiting for me to get up. "I know you do not fear this," he said, without preliminaries, "but I wish I could spare you."

The constraint in his manner brought me sitting upright, with my feet over the edge of the pallet. "The Final Game?" I asked.

He shook his head. "Not yet. Tonight we must question you again—and our methods will be just as severe as necessary to make you answer our questions."

"What do you think you will learn that you couldn't before?" I instinctively sought for words to restrain him.

"I have given it much thought," he answered. "I believe we will learn more this time."

"The truth serum has its limitations," I said. I do not know why I continued to argue. I knew it was useless. But my resistance had been so battered that I think I spoke only to gain time, to postpone what was to come.

"We will try our own methods this time," Trobt answered.

"Torture?" I asked.

His face made a flinching motion, and I knew how much he disliked what he had to do. "I doubt that that will be necessary," he answered. "But if it is, we will use it. In the end you will talk."

The cloak I put about my shoulders covered a far heavier garment.

"I can give you this assurance," Trobt said, as we left the house, "we will harm you no more than we must. We would be cheating both ourselves and you if we made you unfit to die like a man." It was hardly a consolation.

I was not alone with the two men who questioned me. Through a glass wall at the end of the room another dozen watched and listened. I was certain they were in actual charge here. Trobt was among them.

I had only one fatalistic thought, one resolution. That this would be a better time to die than later. At least it would be for a cause. I would give them nothing they could use against my Worlds. I had come into the room prepared not to leave it alive.

My questioners made no pretense of gentleness. They were rough-voiced, and very apparently prepared to be rough-handed if necessary. At the beginning their questions were much the same as under the serum drugging: the power and war potentials of the Ten Thousand Worlds. They threw their questions rapidly, unmercifully, beating at my brain with repetition, going over and over the same ground, hour after hour, asking the same questions, rephrasing them, asking them again. I doubt if they learned much, though. I was not influenced by the drug this time, and they still lacked the background for proper understanding of the answers I gave to mislead them.

They forced me to stand during the ordeal. At first when I tired they gave me brief rests and cool drinks—I was answering the questions they asked. But as it became apparent that they were learning little they gave me no more breaks. They kept me standing and pounded on and on with their questions.

By midnight I was near the end of my endurance. "I need rest," I said.

"Stand!" one of my interrogators barked. He was an ugly, big-trunked man with a scar that smeared the line of his left eyebrow.

I felt the strength flow from my legs.

The big man slapped my face, savagely, with both hands. The wall against my back held me up for a moment as I brushed at his hands, and he drove a fist into my stomach.

I reached for the last ragged threads of my vitality and hit him on the side of the head and he staggered back and fell to the floor. From the corner of one eye I saw the other inquisitor swing a padded weapon at my head, and I had my rest at last.

When consciousness returned I found that I was still on my feet. The inquisitors each held one arm and supported me against the wall. The questions resumed. This time they were different. Perhaps my questioners had been waiting for the sign of weakness I had shown.

"What did you learn in the time you were free in Hearth?" Now they were asking questions about their own side. They would understand the answers I gave.

I shook my head.

The big man released his hold on my arm and struck me on the cheek. "Will we win our war against the Ten Thousand Worlds?"

I shrugged. I could feel with my tongue a gash in the inside of my left cheek.

He hit me twice more, on both sides. "Did you find a weakness?"

Incongruously then I thought of Trobt. I knew his empathy, and that he would be suffering now. I made a special effort not to look at him, for he might take that as a plea for help, and stop this brutality. Which would be ruinous to him. I steeled myself to avoid it.

I watched my tormentor swing his right fist, as though in slow motion, as it came at my head in a powerful overhand drive, with all his strength behind it.

It caught me on the left ear with explosive force, addling my brain and temporarily deafening me. I found that I was sitting on the floor with my back against the wall.

"Answer my question!"

I put my hand to my ear and brought it away smeared with blood. My senses were too addled to answer.

The man grabbed me by the blouse collar, and pulled me to my feet. "Will we win the war?" he repeated.

My hearing was still poor, and I could barely distinguish one word from the other. I heard the answer quite clearly, however.

I had tried with all my strength to hold it back, I would gladly have given my life if I could have stopped it. But I had failed. "Yes," I said.

"Ah—"

I noted then a frightening fact. The annotator—the thing in my mind that was a part of me, and yet apart from me—had assumed control. It had made its motion to take command at the moment I had been beaten into small resistance, and found little opposition.

And I knew the reason it had made its play. It was not concerned with matters of emotion, with sentiments of patriotism, loyalty, honor, and self-respect. It was interested only in my—and its own—survival. Its logic told it that unless I gave the answers my tormentors wanted they would beat me until I did. Until I died, if necessary. And that it had set out to prevent.

I made one last desperate effort to stop that other part of my mind from taking control—and sank lower into my physical and mental impotence.

"What is our weakness?"

Waves of sound coming from within the head itself again blurred my hearing, and I could barely make out the question. "Your society is doomed," I declared.

The annotator had answered again as I stood helpless. And with the answer I understood that I had known it all the while, but that I had never quite resolved it.

"Why?" the questions went on, as I stood with eyes tightly closed.

"There are many reasons."

"Give one."

"Your culture is based on a need to struggle, for combat. When there is no one to fight it must fall."

My questioners were shrewd. They knew the questions to ask now. They were dealing with a familiar culture.

"Explain that."

"Your culture is based on its impetuous need to battle—it is armed and set against dangers and the expectation of danger—fostering the pride of courage under stress. There is no danger now—nothing to fight, no place to spend your over-aggressiveness, except against each other in personal duels. You achieve some measure of sublimation in your Game, but it is not enough. As to your Final Game—that indicates that already your decline is entering the bloody circus and religion stage, already crumbling in the heart while expanding on the outside. And this is your first civilization—you have no experience of a fall in your history before to have recourse to—no cushion of philosophy to accept."

For a time I sensed a puzzled silence in my two tormentors. I doubted that they had the intelligence, or the depth of understanding, to accept the truth and significance of what they heard. However, they were competent men in their job. One of them went over to the glass wall and through a doorway in its side. He returned a few minutes later.

"Is there a solution?" he asked.

"Only a temporary one." Now it was coming.

"Explain."

"War with the Ten Thousand Worlds." I tasted the rusty tang of blood in my mouth as my teeth bit into my tongue.

"Explain."

"Your willingness to hazard, and eagerness to battle is no weakness when you are armed with superior weapons and fighting an opponent as disorganized and as incapable of effective organization as the Ten Thousand Worlds, against your long-range weapons and subtle traps."

"Why do you say the solution is only temporary?"

"You cannot win the war. You will seem to win, but it will be an illusion. You will win battles, kill billions, rape Worlds, take slaves, and destroy ships and armaments. But afterwards you will be forced to hold the subjection. Your numbers will not be expandable. You will be spread thin, exposed to other cultures that will influence you, change you.

"Resistance will rise. You will lose skirmishes, and in the end you will be forced back. Then will come a loss of old ethics. Corruption and opportunism will replace your Honor and you will know shame and dishonor—your society will soon be weltering back into the barbarism and disorganization which in its corruption and despair will be nothing like the proud tribal primitive life of its first barbarism—you will be aware of the change and unable to return."

They maneuvered about that answer for a long time. Going through it again and again. But this time they were not harsh or aggressive. They stopped often and went to the glass wall and returned and asked again, in a different way.

I understood their perplexity. They could not accept what I told them because to them winning was only a matter of military victory, a victory of strength. They had not experienced defeat as a weakness from within. My words only made them uneasy.

The last time one of my questioners returned from the glass partition he asked, "Do we have any other weakness?"

"Your women." Would I never stop? They were picking my brain to defeat my own people.

"Explain."

"They are set for a period when they greatly outnumbered their men. In your early days the men were relatively few in number, reduced by the attrition of fighting the dleeth, and other clans. Your compatible ration was eight women to one man. Now it is one to one, yet you still maintain your tradition of polygamy."

I had to pause for a time, as weariness, and the pain of my battered face threatened to bring a sickness up from my stomach. I breathed deeply, until the nausea lessened.

My questioners had waited patiently. They were wise enough to realize that threats would not hurry my sickness. When they saw I was better, one asked, "What else?"

"I have more on that. The eight-year cycle of your women precludes them from producing the necessary children. Your manpower must ever be in small supply, and there is no way for you to increase it. Worse, the long arid period of the women sponsors a covert despair and sadism in your young men—a hunger and starvation to follow instinct, to win women by courage and conquest and battle against danger."

"The solution?"

"War. Beat the Federation. Be in a position of free access to their women." That should have been apparent to them for quite some time now. Trobt would certainly have thought of it. He had his personal solution with Darlene.

Just before the black walls of oblivion that rimmed my vision closed in, I heard, "That will be enough." Trobt's voice.

I awoke in Trobt's home. I was tired, and extremely weak. The ordeal of the questioning lingered in my mind like fragments of a nightmare coming and going. I felt nothing, for my emotions had not yet been able to work their way through my weariness. I had only the certainty that when they did they would be bitter. I thought of the pain in my body as one huge toothache, numbed only by the inability of my brain to function properly.

Trobt found me in this state of mental and physical stasis. I looked for some sign of triumph, or contempt, in his face, but read neither there.

I was past caring. I felt alone, more alone than I had ever been before. I turned away from him. "You had no power to prevent it," he attempted to console me.

In the space of the next few minutes a queer phantasm passed through my mind. With the realization that I had no slightest hope left came what I recognized as shock. I knew then how a man could be physically unhurt, yet driven so hard that his mind was no longer able to face his depression, until he substituted a false existence for the reality that was too harsh to bear. That way lay madness.

My mind then became coldly logical. As clear, cool, and crisply logical as it is possible for a human mind to be. I began thinking new thoughts, savoring deliciously the wealth of wisdom behind them. I reviewed my past actions, my life, with its aspirations and frustrations, and I saw them as something that I understood fully then for the first time. Philosophies and problems of the universe that had been only dimly comprehended before were easily grasped with an idle passing thought. And too trivial for further contemplation. I had found the supreme wisdom—and the only perfect happiness. Never again would I ever be perplexed or troubled. Before me lay serenity. The serenity of an infinity of knowledge and perception. And behind it all lurked one other bit of understanding: my thoughts were those that only a lunatic would entertain!

Trobt's perspicacity saved me. He had watched me closely those few minutes and now he said, "Only a coward runs."

He had seen what was happening, seen that I was fleeing back into my own mind. That the only way to stop that running was to sting me into staying and fighting.

I hung on grimly.

Two days later I visited Trobt at work.

At the car ramp I found a guard leaning idly against a stone pillar. He smiled as I came up to him. "I will watch you die," he said.

The words were spoken with neither rancor nor hate, but they did irritate. I shrugged. "Is there any reason why I can't leave here?"

"None," he answered, civilly enough. "I'd be happy to drive you anywhere you wish."

My status evidently had changed considerably the last few days. "I'd appreciate that," I said. "Take me to the Games Building, please."

The guard drove with the hairbreadth impetuosity of all the Veldqans.

At the entrance to the Games building a pedestrian snarled as I passed and spat on the ground. "I will watch you die," he grunted. For some reason I seemed to be well-known now. Though hardly well-liked.

We had to go through Lyagin's office to reach the interior of the building. The old man glanced up as I entered behind the guard. He rose when he recognized me and came toward me. "You are a man, sir," he said, smiling an unaccustomed, cracked smile of greeting, and gripping my wrists in feeble hands.

I found myself standing awkwardly, not quite knowing how to respond. His greeting and manner were too unexpected. I had received little respect on this world, and could not easily accept it now. I stammered my thanks.

"Did you know that Yasi and I are—" I began, but the words to finish the sentence failed to come.

He waved away my confusion. "While circumstances may not be normal—" He drifted off into his near senility. He looked up then and his rheumy eyes cleared. "It is possible for an enemy to be worthy, and to be accepted without castigation. You bring honor with you, and will not demean the honor of the Lyagin clan."

I was pleased to hear this, but still uncertain of myself. "You know about... about the Final Game?" I asked hesitantly.

"You will conduct yourself with honor there also."

He was accepting that with considerable equanimity, I thought. I bowed to him, and he gripped my wrists again, and I went on to Trobt's office.

Trobt put down his stylus as I entered and greeted me with the friendliness I had come to expect from him. He indicated a chair and invited me to sit down.

I did not accept the invitation; I was in no mood for perfunctory intercourse. I wanted direct conversation only. "I'd like to know if you still intend to kill me," I said.

"You need have no fear," Trobt answered readily. "We will give you the torture whenever you ask."

He still intended to put me through the ordeal then. I knew by this time that his affection for me was great; I believe that if he could have taken my place, he might have. Yet there was no evidence of his changing his mind.

A new consideration intruded. He had said he would give me the torture whenever I asked. Did that mean. . . . "Are you telling me that you won't send me the Final Game until I decide?" I asked.

"Why would we do that?" Trobt was puzzled now. "There is a period when a man must be allowed to make his preparations, and to bring his mind to a proper order. He will not pass this way again."

And I realized how much there still remained to learn of these people, and how I never would understand them completely. The background necessary for that would take a lifetime of living—as one of them. To know them thoroughly one had to be tied to Veldq by friends, relatives, memories, interests, fears, and hostilities. That I did not have.

Trobt's reply, however, still tantalized me. "What if I postponed it forever?" I asked, in my own mind quite serious.

He smiled as though I had uttered an absurdism. "We both know you won't," he answered.

"How do you know that?" I challenged.

"You wouldn't permit it."

"Do you actually think I'm eager to die?" I asked.

"All Veldq knows you are eager for the Final Game."

"Why?" I asked. "Do they see me as a madman?"

"They see you as you are. They cannot conceive of one man challenging a planet, except to win himself a bright and gory death on a page of history, the first man to deliberately strike and die in the coming war. Not an impersonal clash of battleships, but a *man* declaring battle against men. Every

*   *   *

citizen is waiting to see you die—gloriously. We would not deprive you of that death. Our admiration is too great. We want the symbolism of your blood now just as greatly as you want it yourself."

My mood of introspection had returned as he spoke, and I had just a grasp of what he meant. I had read in the old histories of Earth of a warrior race of North American Indians. A captured enemy must die. But if he had been an honorable enemy he was given an honorable death. He was allowed to die under the stress most familiar to them. Their strongest ethic was a cover-up for the defeated, the universal expressionless suppression of reaction in conquering or watching conquest, so as not to shame the undefeated. Public torture, with the women, as well as the warriors, watching, the chance to exhibit fortitude. That was considered the honorable death, while it was a shameful act quietly to slit a man's throat in his sleep without giving him a chance even to fight, or to show his mettle under torture.

I, however, was not an Indian, or a Veldqan; I was Human, with all my race's strengths and weaknesses, and with its ethics, and I had no wish for Trobt's "honorable" death.

"This dying under torture seems to you to be a very desirable final act," I explained, "but as a Human it seems to me to be only a throwing away of my life. Surely it must have occurred to you that I might refuse to undergo the Final Game, if I had the choice."

Trobt frowned, as though I had told a bad joke. "If a man is a man, there can be no difference, regardless of his race."

"I can't accept that," I answered.

For a moment there was doubt in Trobt's expression, and possibly scorn. "If you are serious, think on it a moment," he stated, very seriously. "Think on what would happen if you refused. At first no one would believe you, our people would consider it some jest or twist of alien character, but as time went by and you remained alive, they would begin to doubt, until they gradually became convinced that you were a coward, and they would begin to despise you. You would be subjected to increasing scorn, be spat upon, until finally they would slit your throat—as you would deserve. Would that be a better way to die?"

Trobt still lacked the ability to understand that the strong ethics of his race did not apply to mine, and I suspected that I had no arguments that could convince him. Yet he may have been right here.

"That would not be a better way to die," I found myself answering him, and knew I had made a new resolution. Trobt had convinced me that if I had to die, it would be better to die as a man than as a coward.

I dismissed the subject then, as my mind drifted to something Trobt had said earlier. From the time I had been captured in the City I'd suspected that he had allowed me to escape, deliberately. He had lured me to a different maze test, allowing me the freedom to search, to learn all I could about the Veld-gans. After which they had subjected me to the torture questioning, to turn my newly gained knowledge to their advantage. They would learn how to make themselves stronger, and how to defend themselves against us by what they learned from me.

Also, my own actions and reactions must have given them a better understanding of their opponent in the upcoming duel of races, so that in exposing myself, and the strengths and weaknesses of my kind, they would be better able to confront us. Through Trobt's intelligence, and skill, I had lost any advantage I might have had here originally.

Yet I was not completely disconsolate. I still had one resource remaining—an extremely vital one. The twitch-tape. And with my new freedom I should be able to find a power source—and send my report back to the Worlds. That would be of great value to them, and almost make up for what I had lost here.

Trobt had implied he suspected I might have a means of communicating with my Worlds, but had not been able to discover what it was. Undoubtedly his only failure.

"I would like to show you something that I'm certain will interest you," Trobt said then, apparently in an effort to regain our good relationship, which had been quite severely strained the past few minutes. He led the way to a window, and we looked out at a silent, intense crowd, filling every square yard of a large courtyard and spilling out into the street. They all seemed to be staring at the wall just beneath us. "What are they doing there?" I asked.

"They are watching a vision screen set in the wall," Trobt answered. "The courtyard has been crowded all day, and there are hundreds of other screens about the City, all as crowded with spectators as this one."

"What do they watch?"

"If you will follow me?" Trobt led the way through a corridor, down a ramp, and out a side door of the building. We stood in the doorway, at the edge of the crowd, where we were able to see the vision screen Trobt had mentioned, set high up on the building.

On it showed a group of citizens, surrounding two in the center. One was short and stocky, the other deep-chested and bearded. Both held short knives in their right hands. And both were blindfolded!

There was a brief flurry of sudden movement from the two in the center, and the shorter fell back clutching his neck where it met his left shoulder. Blood poured out from between his fingers.

The crowd in the courtyard muttered and gave brief cheers. Here and there voices called, "A wounded dleeth! He walks big! He will go far in the Final Game! I will watch!"

The bearded man, of course, was I.

I turned to Trobt. "What is this?" I asked.

"We had scanners everywhere when you escaped. Only at rare intervals were you out of our sight."

"You did allow me to escape, then?"

"Of course. I thought that by this time you would understand that."

"I guessed," I said. "And the pictures?"

"They are a transcript of your actions during the time you were free in Hogarth."

It had not been unexpected. This man had surprised me too often with his brilliant handling of me—and my situation—for me to be taken aback now. "Did the Veldqans know that you had deliberately allowed me to escape?"

"They didn't while you were in the City, but they do now. The transcript has been shown repeatedly since. Yet they watch with undiminished fascination. Even parts such as your sleeping under the City, they watch with as much interest as if they were witnessing a great drama."

Someone in the crowd at our side said, "I will watch him die!"

"Why do they hate me?" I asked Trobt.

"What you just heard was a compliment," Trobt answered. "Some do hate you, naturally. They hate you as the representative of their enemy. But to the great majority you are a hero. The entire planet admires you, for you are the enemy who came to challenge. Alone. The test champion come to precede the battle, the best contesting the best. And so they will wait eagerly for the time when you will fight to maintain your race's honor. I'm certain they will not only observe but cheer your every advance in the Final Game."

Here was that unshakable viewpoint again.

"You have captured the imagination of all," Trobt said. "When you die in the manner I know you must, you will undoubtedly become the greatest enemy-hero in the history of Veldq."

I was a hero. Yet they would kill me.

9

That night I dreamed of the Veldqans. I was surrounded by thousands of them, all speaking at the same time, shouting at me, explaining themselves, in jumbled, broken phrases:

Honor . . . courage . . . birthright . . . inherited . . . old survival traits . . . the world belongs to the strong . . . love danger . . . not only to desire. . . . Danger . . . harshness . . . violence . . . war . . . valuable factors . . . progress. . . . Must be passionate. Without it . . . impotence. Weaklings and inefficients must perish. Struggle . . . existence . . . strong will survive. Weak must . . . society must excrete . . . defectives . . . must not be allowed . . . or strength departs.

I awoke bathed in perspiration.

That afternoon a visitor brightened my day.

Yasi. How precious that name had become to me.

I had not forgotten her, even with all that had been happening the past few days, and the cool sweetness of her smile and her kiss brought back a flood of tenderness.

Trobt and I found her waiting in his game room when we entered. He smiled now at our joyful meeting. Yasi, however, had attention only for me. "Observe," she commanded me, once again parading herself for my inspection. Thankfully this time she did not shed her clothing.

The burgeoning of her womanhood was quite apparent in her body, and in the creamy pinkness that had begun to blossom in her cheeks. She was not yet quite a complete woman. She reminded me of an Earth girl, in secondary school, pert, vivacious, and just beginning to recognize her imminent chrysalis. She would very soon be as much woman as any man could ask for—or cope with.

"Do you find me pleasing, Leonard Stromberg?" she asked, with a kind of singing in her voice.

I answered by taking both her hands in mine and letting her read in my eyes what I felt about her. At that moment I was as happy as I could be on this alien world.

"Why then did you not return to me?" Yasi questioned. "Is it that you do not think me proper?" She turned appealingly to Trobt. "Will you tell him that I am worthy?"

Trobt was enjoying my inability to keep up with her conversational sprightliness. He nodded solemnly, however. "She is the youngest of Lyagin Concor, of the clan of Lyagin. They are long an honorable family of Veldq." In one of his rare assays at humor, "By our standards she is considered very beautiful."

He knew by the look in my eyes how much I agreed with that assessment. "I consider you a most fortunate man," Trobt said.

"And so you see?" Yasi demanded.

"Yasi. Yasi." I folded her slim body in my arms. "I needed no one to vouch for you. To me you are everything that is wonderful." I was very sincere, and not at all deterred by Trobt's presence.

This time it was Yasi who was quiet, but I could feel her very much alive, and happy, in her supple body.

Trobt left us then, and we spent the afternoon together. For that time all cares left me.

That evening when we'd finished our leisurely meal, Trobt retired to his room, while I took my usual exercise in the garden. Yasi's having to leave earlier had left me in a particularly gloomy mood, partially I knew, because I was homesick.

I badly wanted to visit my old home town, St. Paul, Minnesota, to sing in a barbershop quartet, to watch Bill and Connie Carroll dance a rhumba to Johnny Reynold's band.

Added to that was a strong sense of foreboding. Not an anticipation of the Final Game, but I was concerned about Trobt's mannerisms and conversation during our evening meal.

When he came into the garden carrying two goblets of dark Veldqan wine, and an oilskin packet under one arm, and a disarming smile on his face, I was not deceived. Something there was not quite right, I knew.

"Veldq's finest wine," Trobt said, placing one goblet in front of me and pouring blood-red wine into it. "Tell me what you think of its bouquet."

I tested it, finding it a bit bitter for my taste, but was not discourteous enough to mention it.

"Will you drink an Earthian toast with me?" Trobt asked, raising his goblet. Something in his manner still disconcerted me, but when he proposed a straightforward, "To mutual respect," and drained his glass, I followed his example.

Trobt refilled our glasses, and a short while later opened the packet he had brought with him and took out several small bottles. They were labeled, I noticed, with Earthian writing. "I purchased these drugs while visiting your Worlds," he said. "I thought they might possibly be of value to us. If you are familiar with them, perhaps you will explain their usage to me."

I checked them over, recognizing many. "These are called aspirin," I said, indicating a larger bottle I'd picked up. "They ease pain."

Trobt shook his head. "They would be of little interest to us." His reaction was the same for the other pain killers and relief medicines.

One drug, a powdery white pill with a D stamped on it, puzzled me for a moment, until I read the instructions, and saw that it was one of the hallucinogenic drugs. "This one is called a 'dreamer,'" I explained to Trobt. "It puts a user into a trance-like state, deluding him into believing that he is undergoing some experience that he very much enjoys. Probably something he has always wanted to do. It's illegal on most of the Worlds."

"Why is that?" I was surprised to find that I had Trobt's absorbed attention.

"They're dangerous," I said. "You don't do anything harmful to yourself while under their influence; you don't walk over a cliff, or cut your veins. It's more what you don't do that can cause the damage, and why they're banned on most Worlds. In the dream you think you've eaten a sumptuous banquet, or slept, or drunk your fill, when you haven't. Then an auxiliary effect of the drug takes over and your body mechanism reacts as though you had eaten or drunk or slept. Which can be worse than mere inconvenience. Continuous use of the pill will not only disarrange your life, but it can kill you as well. You die of thirst, or hunger, or even lack of rest."

The remaining drugs seemed to have only meager interest for Trobt, and he left me a short while later, and retired to his room, while I sat back in my lounge chair, quite relaxed, and feeling carefree and content. For some unexplainable reason my earlier gloom had vanished.

Until, gradually, almost as though I were waking from a light sleep, I became aware of a long ski slide at the rear of the garden. It was covered with authentic-appearing snow, and a skier was crouched low as he rushed down the steep slope. He hurtled off the end of the slide, hung poised for an instant, and landed on a long sloping hill. I was reminded of a scene at the Iron Mountain, Michigan, winter resort, where Earth's championship skiing trials were held—and abruptly it *was* Iron Mountain, and *I* was the skier, setting a new world record!

The transition had been so subtle that even as one part of my mind recognized the absurdity of the skiing illusion, the other accepted it as real—and reveled in its sheer pleasure. I had always enjoyed winter sports, and had won several trophies in my youth, but of late years I had indulged only occasionally. Yet buried in my subconscious must still linger the dream of a championship.

At that instant a stabbing emotion triggered an alarm in my brain: a consternation at the realization that I had been duped—was at that moment certainly defenseless—vulnerable to any design Trobt might have on me.

It was the word "dream" that had loosed my understanding of what had happened. Trobt had put a dream pill into my wine while we talked. The man's ingenuity had no limits. At first thought it seemed a sly act, not worthy of him, but on second thought I realized that to a man as devoted to his world as Trobt nothing would deter him.

Of more immediate moment now was that I must swiftly gather all my resources to block Trobt's maneuver. My knowledge of the dream pellets was limited, but I suspected that if I could bring sufficient concentration to bear I'd be able to banish this one's illusion—for a limited time at least. I set my mind first to the skiing outfit I appeared to be wearing, and was gratified to observe the clothing fade and my Veldqan suit reappear. Next, I gave my intent regard to the ski slide, and the snow, and watched as they became an ephemeral haze and disappeared.

I rose carefully then, keeping my attention on my real surroundings, not letting them slide into the miasma hovering on the edges of my vision. The ski slide threatened to reappear, and a helicopter sputtered overhead, discharging a hovering sky diver, but I banished them with the force of my will.

What I needed, very urgently, I decided, was a doctor. I walked gingerly from the house.

Outside, I walked through Hearth's almost deserted streets toward the doctor's office the guardian and I had visited. I was in a near daze. I had difficulty keeping my eyes in focus, and all about me the houses, sidewalks, pedestrians, had acquired a strange unreality, had grown elongated and flattened out, become bleached and faded. I treaded my way through them with a high-stepping care.

Somewhere along the route I must have taken a wrong turn, for the buildings gradually thinned out, and only a short time later I found myself alone, treading resolutely through coarse red sand, across a red plain. I stopped and looked about, searching for the way back to the city, but the road had vanished.

I drew in a deep breath, feeling my taut-muscled shoulders pressing against my warrior harness. For a moment I rested my right hand on the hilt of the great-bladed sword at my side, experiencing a reassurance at the cool feel of the leather-bound grip in my hand.

I gazed about over the desolate landscape surrounding me, and directly ahead spied the walls of a mighty city. Without hesitation I set off toward it with long powerful strides. Somehow I knew that it was there they had taken the Red Princess. I had sworn by the all-powerful God of the Rugged Mountain that I would rescue her. Only death could stay that resolve.

The walls that had appeared so substantial from the distance proved on closer inspection to be crumbled and broken. I passed through a gap left by a fallen section into the shadowed city, my steps echoing dully on the rough stone street. Directly overhead a startled bat-bird squawked hoarsely and spread huge featherless wings and sailed off into the distance.

A muted scream came from a dilapidated edifice to my left and I spun around just in time to see two huge blue men carry a struggling burden through a dim doorway. I could not make out what they carried, but did catch a glimpse of a red feminine arm fluttering over a blue shoulder before they disappeared.

They had the Red Princess!

I growled deep in my mighty chest and sprinted toward the low structure, my Earth muscles covering the ground in great thirty-foot bounds.

The inside of the building proved to be nothing more than the gaping mouth of a wide tunnel. The Princess's captors had nowhere to go except down the tunnel, I saw, and I followed swiftly. Radium lights, set high in walls five thousand years old, still retained their power, and lit my way as I ran.

A hundred yards into the passageway an iron gate closed in my face. On a side wall I spied the controls that operated the gate—but the way to them was blocked by an ancient guardsman. "If you would pass, you must produce the countersign," he declared.

"Ancient one," I intoned earnestly. "I have no countersign, but my mission is more vital than life itself, and you must allow me through the portal."

"None shall pass without the proper credentials," the guardian intoned adamantly.

"My time is too precious to waste in argument," I said sternly. "You will permit me through or I must take your life."

The ancient guardsman chuckled and drew his sword, a wicked weapon with a shining steel blade ornamented with finely wrought figures. It must have been fashioned by a craftsman of exceptional skill for it was a weapon as formidable as my own great sword.

"Try me, fool," the guardian cackled.

We clashed swords, swiftly and skillfully, with the sounds of our blows rebounding from the crumbling walls and echoing hollowly down the long tunnel. The ancient one proved to be a surprisingly staunch foe, a swordsman with unexpected expertise and dexterity. So great was the old one's proficiency that I suspected he must belong to the legendary Society of Sword Masters. I had never met this one's equal in any of a thousand sword battles in my past.

Nevertheless the Sword Master was not quite able to cope with the blade that had carved its way across half a continent in its pursuit of the captors of the Red Princess, and he died, gamely.

I pressed the gate controls then and when the portal opened went through and set off down the tunnel with long distance-devouring strides. The way seemed endless, but at last I came to a gently ascending slope and followed it until it opened into the ruined city again.

And there I overtook the villains!

They had heard me coming, and one, a blue giant near eight feet tall, roughly tossed the girl he carried against the nearest wall. The Princess cried out once, then was still, her fair body crumpled on the ground.

I muttered a curse under my breath and pulled out the great sword. Nothing would save them now. The blue giants died within one minute of our engagement.

I had stooped to rescue the still form of the Princess when I heard, coming from the passageway behind us, the thunder of rapidly approaching feet. I spun about and saw at least fifty of the blue giants advancing swiftly, too many even for my mighty weapon.

My agile brain made an instant decision. There was one chance, and one chance only. If Tars Tarkas had been successful in reaching the city—and if he had kept our appointment.

I bent and picked up the Princess, pausing for only a brief instant to cherish the warmth of her dear form against my chest before I carried her swiftly out into the courtyard.

Ahead a twenty-foot-high wall blocked our way. Too high for me to reach with the burden I bore. My only hope was a performance greater than any I had ever called upon from my magnificent sinews. Breaking into a gradually accelerating run, I gathered every last ounce of strength in my powerful Earth muscles—and leaped upward.

The light gravity of this world, and my superbly conditioned body, had often in the past enabled me to perform feats impossible to the native born, but here I was asking more than bone and flesh could deliver. I did not reach my objective.

However, I did succeed in reaching the edge of the wall, and I swung out my free arm and grasped the far side—and with a supreme effort pulled myself and the Princess up and onto the top.

Spending not a second to savor my triumph I strode to the outer edge of the barricade and gazed down. In the shadows forty feet below a great-bodied green giant—seated on one supple-legged throt, and holding the reins of a second—waved a green hand. Faithful Tars Tarkas had not failed me. I girded my loins, aimed for the back of the nearest throt—with the Princess still in my arms—and leaped.

A faint glimmer of reason, as of a light shining through a small opening, penetrated my fogged brain, and I realized that I had been sucked into the dream world of my subconscious. I struggled with all my will to pull myself out.

10

I was abruptly back on the streets of Hearth, standing in front of the building that held the doctor's office. Trobt put in a shadowy appearance, incongruously seated on a chair in the middle of the street, but I blinked swiftly, twice, and he disappeared.

I blinked a third time—and I was standing in the hall of the medical clinic on the third floor. What a wonderful form of transportation I've discovered, I thought, with amusement.

The clinic door was locked, but a sign directed me to the end of the hall where a small anteroom was lit dimly. I went in and by the muted light of a vision screen could make out the doctor who had dressed my wounded arm a few weeks before. He was seated in an easy chair, watching the screen, where a bearded man played a Game with a melon merchant. Myself again. Evidently these were a repetitious, easily entertained people.

The doctor was dozing, I saw, and I shook him by the shoulder. He opened his eyes and looked up at me through thick bubbles of his eye glasses.

The room made an attempt to expand, and the vision screen became a face, that guffawed silently, but I glared it back to normalcy. "Someone fed me a dreamer pill," I explained to the doctor. "I need an antidote."

The request aroused only small reaction. "Then how do you know I'm not an illusion?" he asked, smiling broadly at his intended joke.

At that particular moment his wry humor amused me not at all. "I'll just have to hope you're not an illusion," I answered.

"You understand that the user of a dream pill can't distinguish between reality and illusion?" the doctor asked. "Even after the effects of the drug have worn off he can't be certain that what he remembers really happened, or if he dreamed it."

I did not answer. I was in the midst of a struggle to hold back a large blue wave that washed out from one wall, threatening to carry me and the physician out to sea.

"The best way to judge whether or not you're dreaming is to check just how much you're enjoying yourself." The doctor apparently was a conversation addict. "The pills give wish fulfillments, you know, so if you very much like what you're experiencing, you're probably dreaming."

I had been holding myself stiffly erect, and now I felt a hot flush envelop me, and I noted that my body was covered with a tepid perspiration. I was definitely not enjoying this. The blue wave reappeared and sprayed me with a cool invigorating spray. Enjoyed, therefore illusion.

"If you have an antidote, I'll need it fast," I informed the doctor. My vision blurred again, and I reached for a nearby table to steady myself, but my hand passed through the table, and I staggered and almost lost my balance.

"Here, sit down—before you fall down." The doctor rose and indicated the easy chair he had vacated. He walked quickly toward a rear wall covered with high glass door panels. "I suppose I talk too much," he apologized as he reached up and opened a glass door and took down two bottles and began measuring out white powders and pouring them into a widemouthed beaker.

I had a moment of doubt. This office was much better equipped, and supplied, with its long shelves of medical ingredients, than I had noted on my first visit. I hadn't thought

the Veldqans would use this many drugs. I decided quickly
that I needed the doctor's help too much to question it now.

"One other thing you should be warned about," the doctor
said, as he added a liquid to the powders in the beaker. "You're
pretty helpless when you're under the drug. You can be robbed,
or hurt, and not even be aware—"

He had completed the preparation of the antidote by this
time, and he stood with it in his hand now, distracted by his
own conversation.

The counter behind him became a belt, covered with small
white pellets, moving as on an assembly line, and the rows of
pills grew higher, some of them spilling to the floor. Dimly
I wondered what wish this was fulfilling, but when the pills
gradually changed to snow, and the belt became a ski slide,
I understood. I closed my eyes, holding the lids tightly closed
for an instant, opened them again, and walked over and took
the beaker from the doctor's hand.

"Oh, I'm sorry," he said. "Talking too much again."

I drank deeply.

In a matter of only a few seconds I experienced an immense
relief. No more illusions, no more fighting to hold back pleasure fantasies.

And I found myself out in the street again, remembering
only then that I had forgotten either to thank or pay the doctor.
I debated going back, but my feet carried me ahead, and I
decided against it. I'd stop in again some other time.

A small doubt came to mind then. The doctor . . . I thought
I remembered that there were no doctors on Veldq. And he
had been wearing bubble glasses. I had never seen a Veldqan
wearing glasses. Could it be possible that he had visited the
Worlds also . . .

I found myself climbing the ramp to Trobt's home, and
understood only then where I had been heading. My subconscious was assuming part control now, which pleased me. It
had always served me well in the past.

Abruptly a newborn plan, scintillating and exquisite in its
breadth and profundity, flashed through into the conscious
portion of my mind. It was not yet exact in all its formulations
but its very scope and effectiveness of purpose brought an

exhilarating joy of creation. This was one of those inspirations that come to a man once, if at all, in a lifetime.

I found Trobt waiting for me in his game room. "Come in, my friend," he invited—after the fact.

We *were* friends, which should make my mission easier. "I'd like to speak to your Council," I told him.

Trobt's eyebrows raised.

"I have what I'll call a proposition," I said. "Of extreme importance. That will have to be decided by your highest government body."

Trobt shifted his stylus from one side of his desk to the other, a small sign of impatience. "That won't be necessary," he said evenly. "I'll be quite able to judge whether or not any proposition you have will interest them."

I had noticed before that his authority seemed greater than the Council's but I was feeling quite officious at that moment. "I'm not asking for an opinion," I asserted. "I want an agreement—a binding agreement—or a rejection, if they should see it that way."

"I won't pretend that my word would be all you'd need." Trobt hesitated, then said decisively "I'll call them." He went across the room to the Veldqan version of a vision master and gripped the handles on its side. "This is Kalin Trobt," he said to the person on the other end. "Contact the Council, and have them meet at my home. Immediately." He paused. "Yes, yes, I realize that. Yes, call them." He returned to his chair opposite me.

I must have taken a short nap. When I opened my eyes the Council members were there, seated in a row facing me. They were all dressed exactly alike, brown boots and wraparound leggings, short tan trousers and leather coats. Even their thin-cheeked faces looked alike, as though they were all of the same family, and all wore identical expressions of melancholic passivity. I restrained a chuckle with difficulty.

Trobt gave no explanations or preliminary comments, merely nodded to me.

"I won't ask whether or not you men know my purpose on your world," I began. "If you don't, you soon will. For now, permit me to bring to your attention certain studies that have been undertaken by astral observers on our Ten Thousand Worlds." At that point I paused, to review in my mind one last time the order, and the stress, I would give my arguments, solemnly aware of the significance of what I was about to propose. This might represent a momentous turn in the destiny of both our races.

"Our Ten Thousand Worlds, as you may or may not know," I began again, "are located on the outer edge of our spiral arm of the galaxy—yours is some distance in toward the center of the arm.

"Several generations ago an observer group on one of our Worlds caught signals which indicated that a vast civilization, considerably larger than our Ten Thousand Worlds, existed in a star group just to your side of the spiral arm. The studies continued and expanded through the years, and those first signals have been verified. Further, subsequent data indicates that the race is expanding rapidly. Our best judgment is that they will reach the Worlds within two hundred years, Veldq, being closer, will be reached before then.

"Sociological students agree that only an advanced civilization, of a much higher level than either of ours, could expand that rapidly. Concomitantly, such an advanced people would have a greatly superior technology, with superior machines and weapons. The students postulate that they would be warlike, and brook no opposition to their advance.

"Therefore, we must accept the conclusion that their progress will continue, and that in a comparatively short time we will have to fight them.

"Now!" Their eyes widened in group question, as I deliberately sharpened their attention. "Veldq is between that virile race and the Ten Thousand Worlds. They will reach you first, and you will be the first to suffer their onslaught. I know you have great confidence in your own powerful weapon, but you'd be fools not to expect theirs to be as good or better—and you would never be able to withstand their assault. And the numbers—" I thought to startle them with a statistic. "Do you realize that there are probably more children born on their worlds every day than comprise your entire population?" I paused, and the heads all swiveled toward Trobt.

"What would you suggest?" he asked me quietly.

"That for the good of both of us, we unite," I told him.

As he hesitated, I added, "If those long-range considerations don't convince you, consider your immediate advantages. Veldq would—by the necessity of its location—be the first line of defense. The Worlds would pour in an unlimited amount of money to arm you, and to construct defenses. You would quickly be the most prosperous planet in our union, every man woman and child on Veldq would benefit." I stopped talking then. If I hadn't convinced them by that time there was no point in my trying any further arguments.

Trobt spoke again, still hesitantly. "I don't mean to offend," he said, "but in a matter this grave, we'd have to have some proof of what you've told us. Can you furnish that proof?"

I considered, at some length, and had another inspiration. "I have, of course, no proof to give you," I said. "However, I can offer you something so valuable that you'd know I would not give it unless I was very sincere."

"And that is?" Trobt questioned.

"Buried somewhere inside me," I said, "is a nerve-twitch tape on which I've recorded information and impressions of your planet. They would be very valuable to our Worlds in understanding you. To send them back I'd need a quite powerful energy source. Barring that, it would be accomplished by my death. Flesh pockets of chemicals are buried in my body also. If my temperature drops fifteen degrees below normal the chemicals will be activated and will use the tissues of my body for fuel, and generate sufficient energy to transmit the information on the tape back to the Ten Thousand Worlds."

"Thank you," Trobt said. "We will consider what you have told us."

The interview had ended considerably quicker than I'd expected. I would have thought that they'd question me longer. My words must have made a deep impression.

I left the meeting with Trobt and the government officials, extremely satisfied with the night's work, and quickly went to sleep on my pallet—only mildly disturbed by the long ski slide that began to take shape on the far side of the room just before I closed my eyes.

* * *

Trobt woke me early the next morning, his manner condoling. "I hope you are feeling well," he greeted.

I didn't answer, realizing that he had more to say.

"I could not believe your story of the superior civilization, of course," he continued then. "There were just too many discrepancies. You will recognize them yourself, now that you are no longer under the influence of the dream drug."

I'd swear that at the time I'd talked to Trobt and his Council—had the Council actually been there, I wondered abstractedly, and decided it had not—I had myself believed the story of the superior civilization threatening us. It was small consolation to realize now that it had been a figment of my drugged state.

But... the twitch-tape.... I felt nothing concerning my revelation of the tape, for my emotions had not yet been able to work their way up through my weariness. I had only the certainty that when they did my reactions would be bitter.

At that moment I felt alone, more alone than I had ever been before. I tried to sit up, and the muscles of my chest protested violently. I looked up at Trobt. "You operated?" I asked.

"Yesterday," he concurred, revealing to me that more time had passed than I'd realized. "You were kept under Human anaesthetic drugs while the twitch-tape and chemicals were removed from your body." When I continued to do no more than stare at him, he said, "They were buried in the flesh in the front of and below your left shoulder socket."

My first emotion reached the surface then. Despair. And with it fled any last hope I might have had. Before, when the situation had seemed hopeless, I had had the consolation of knowing that my death would at least benefit the Ten Thousand Worlds. Now even that was gone. I had left only the nauseating knowledge that I was the worst kind of traitor.

Trobt did what he could. "Sleep," he said, "and repair yourself." He left me then.

I did not see Trobt again for two days. I had spent the time in a near mental stasis, in a numbness that left me without interest in anything around me.

When Trobt returned he tried to talk to me, without response, and read the signs, and said, "Will you dress, please. I would like you to ride with me."

I obeyed, and we went out and rode a tricar through a gate in the wall of Hearth, on the opposite side from where I had discovered the truck train. We followed the River Widd for perhaps six or seven miles, until we came to a place where it spilled over the bank of a deep gorge. The volume of water and the depth of its fall caused it to hit the bottom of the gorge with a high rise of spray, and a vibration we could feel in the soles of our feet.

"This is my favorite spot, when I want to think or just relax." Trobt had to raise his voice to make himself heard over the roar of the waterfall. "My cares always seem far away when I am here."

I could understand that, but at the moment it interested me not at all.

"A man does not always have to win a fight to be successful," Trobt said. "If he has fought well, given his best without flinching, he has done all that can be asked of a man."

I remained silent.

"I don't know just how much you have learned about us," he tried another tack, "but part of our racial philosophy can best be described as, 'It is as easy for the strong to be strong as it is for the weak to be weak.'"

Despite my dreary state I found myself considering what he had said. My insatiable curiosity could not be stifled entirely.

"You do not praise a strong man because he can lift a heavy weight, and berate a weaker one because he cannot. All we ask is that each do what he can."

Another small facet of this culture's makeup was being revealed here, and ordinarily I would have been extremely interested, but now my attention held for only a scant minute— and my mind retreated again.

"Consider this then—" Trobt seemed to be doing everything he could to alleviate my pain. "You consider us barbarians, I know. Yet we are not sadistic, and we have no thirst for anyone's blood. If we are successful in our war against the Humans, we will not seek pillage or slaughter or noncombatants. We will make every effort to restrain violence. All we wish is to erase the insult to which you have subjected us."

He looked for some response from me, but when he received none, added, "If you know of some way to lessen the suffering that is inevitable, I will gladly listen."

He had not succeeded in penetrating my dejection, but I felt the annotator make a note of his words. Perhaps in the future. . . .

"Then there is only one remedy remaining," Trobt at last stopped trying to talk me out of my mood. "I will take you to the only place where you can be healed."

We rode back to the city, with me not even remotely interested in our new destination. Even when he stopped at Yasi's home. I should have been surprised, and pleased, but my emotions remained dormant, I doubted then that they would ever awaken.

Yasi met us with concern, reading immediately my condition. "What have you done to him?" she questioned Trobt fiercely.

"He has been wounded in the mind only," Trobt answered. "You should be able to make him well." He made his escape then.

Yasi made me sit at a table, and quickly prepared a meal, which I ate without interest. She ate also, almost ravenously— I had noted before that her burgeoning msst had brought with it a great appetite—but she observed my every bite, with the wide-open guileless eyes of a newborn antelope, and when I finished she led me to her bedroom. There she undressed me, and made me get into her bed. I was little more than an automaton, ready to follow anyone's command, and I obeyed, but afterward I lay unmoving, gazing blankly at the nearest wall.

Yasi undressed then, with impatient haste, and crawled into the bed with me. She curled her supple body close against mine, limb pressing limb, her breasts and rounded middle warming my back, and her tears wetting my shoulder.

I had not thought that I could ever be so emotionally drained that in circumstances such as that I would not respond to a beautiful woman—or perhaps even to one not so beautiful— and yet this was Yasi, to me all that was mysterious and fascinating in woman, and I cared not at all that she shared the bed with me.

With her woman's wisdom Yasi said nothing, waiting for the miracle of her womanhood to exert its magic and break the spell. Even then I might have remained unresponsive except that as our bodies warmed, the delicate scent of her msst enveloped us, exerting a strong insistent pull at my resistance, that soon worked its way through the stasis—and I could no longer remain indifferent. I turned to face her, and began exploring and fondling that sweet, delightful body, that by now had developed all its charms of sensuous femininity.

Yasi responded in kind, kissing me hungrily, and murmuring small excited phrases that quickened the hormones in my blood, and gradually a great all-pervasive hunger grew in my loins. I covered her then, and entered her, urgently but tenderly—and the moment grew suddenly still, as though the realities in which we moved had paused. They began again when we loved, tranquilly, I still with great gentleness, and at the end I knew that I would never love another woman.

Later we made love again, this time fiercely and passionately, and my affection increased, if that was possible.

As we lay enclosed in the warm satisfaction of our completion, I said, "We'll be married as soon as possible."

Yasi laughed lightly, and said, "When I entered your bed, we were married."

"We were?" I could only think to repeat.

"It is by the laws." She pulled herself over onto me and gazed down at me possessively. "On Veldq it is the woman who decides," she pronounced, enjoying the declaration of control, but with no real selfishness. "Never has a man been known to refuse, when a Veldqan woman chooses him," she said. "I hope that is not difficult for you to understand," she had her fun with me.

It was certainly not difficult to understand why a man would be unable to resist such an advance, I considered, but there was the question of how permanent such a marriage would be. Until I recalled that there was no Veldqan word for divorce. Apparently the women had an instinct for proper choice also.

Our love was so great that that would be no concern of

ours, I thought smugly, and made my own innocuously sly plan.

In the morning Yasi and I bathed together in her rock basin, washing each other's bodies, and playing and splashing water, and laughing all the while, like children.

Afterward Yasi prepared breakfast for us, a substantial gruel of some species of grain, which she thinned with the bittersweet milk. It tasted surprisingly good, but I had only a small appetite, and I occupied myself watching with amusement as Yasi devoured her meal with a kind of genteel gluttony. Her metabolism demanded sustenance, I knew, so that it could fulfill its mission of msst.

Still in the nude, Yasi cleared our breakfast places, and I inspected all the changes that had taken place in her—in a short nineteen days. All her body had fleshed out, not moderately, but to a degree I would not have believed possible, had I not witnessed it.

Her breasts could best be described by the adolescent expression, "super-bloopers," though that is too irreverent a term for Yasi's delights. From her breasts her body tapered to the hips, and swelled out again, broad and strong—shaped to bear her race's robust and virile offspring—and culminating in delicious buttocks that rivaled those of the nudes of Ingres. There was so much compelling femininity there that I gazed at it with a kind of unbelieving shyness.

She was fat, I had to admit it, yet it was in no way a grossness, only the ripening of woman in all her female glory. She reminded me of adolescents of the Caribbean races, who reach their full-fleshed fruition while still young. The fact that many of them would so quickly grow loose-fleshed and heavy of body, detracted not at all from that youthful desirability. Further, as someone has asked, how many fat old maids do you see?

Yasi, of course, would not grow heavier, but would in time return to her boy-girl shape.

When Yasi and I had finished washing our dishes and putting them away, I kissed her, and left the house on my sly mission, leaving her mystified, but never uncertain of my returning.

Trobt would not be home, I knew, but it was not him I sought. His plump wife, Darlene, listened to my story with shining eyes, and promised to do everything I asked. Still very mysterious, I returned to Yasi and had her prepare to leave. I helped her on with her cloak, and she accompanied me from the house with anticipation as well as great curiosity.

Darlene and Trobt waited for us with, to my considerable surprise, Yasi's father, Lyagin. It was very proper that he should be here, I reflected immediately, contrite that I had not thought of it myself. I was thankful for Darlene's more acute sense of correct form.

The old fellow was dressed in a black fur outfit, with a high collar—that must have been uncomfortably warm, I couldn't help thinking—which I guessed was formal attire here. He said nothing, but kept bobbing his head at me, which I took for approval.

Darlene led Yasi into her dressing room, while Trobt and Lyagin and I stood about, awkwardly making small talk. Here, as on Earth, males always feel lost in those social activities, while conversely, the ladies always seem so thoroughly self-assured.

Finally Darlene and Yasi emerged, with Yasi dressed all in white, as an Earth bride would be, and so beautiful that for an instant I feared she could not be real. I stood frozen, lost in the marvel of her.

Lyagin went to her side and took her arm, looking at Darlene questioningly, and she nodded, reassuring him, I supposed, that he was following her instructions properly. She looked toward Trobt, but he seemd to have no doubts about his duties. She would have briefed him thoroughly on Human weddings, I was certain, probably having insisted on one herself.

Trobt cleared his throat, and I came to attention, and stepped in front of him, and proudly received Yasi from her father. "Will you love and cleave to this woman for all time?" Trobt asked me, and all the rest of the ceremony is lost to my memory, for I had no attention other than for Yasi.

Darlene kissed us both at the end, crying unabashedly, while we men hugged the women, and each other—without hesitation or self-consciousness. I thought I saw tears in Lyagin's eyes also.

As we prepared to leave, Trobt said, "Take all the time you wish." It was meant as a kindness, but I could not fail to perceive that nothing had changed there. I was still expected to. . . . I refused to think about it then.

11

Two men whom I recognized as Trobt's guards drove our tricars. Yasi and I sat in one, Lyagin in the other.

"We go for Father's courting of my new mem-mother," Yasi explained, and at my uncomprehending look, expanded on the statement. "My mother is dead, and in such a circumstance one of my mem-mothers would take her place, but all four of them have died also. Therefore he must court another."

"What are mem-mothers?" I asked.

"The other wives of Lyagin," she returned. "They were my mem-mothers."

"They are all dead, and he is going to court another one?" I asked, trying to get some understanding of what was going on here, and knowing I was about to learn another custom of these people.

"It is a formality only," Yasi said.

I took her by the shoulders and turned her toward me. "Start at the beginning," I demanded with mock sternness.

Yasi sighed, which occasioned a delightful rise of her splendid breasts, and made me lose the tenor of my inquiry.

"It is the duty of the bride's mother and father to guard when the young people who are to be united enter the cave for their Genesis Time," Yasi said.

She had answered one question, but introduced two others. "What do you mean by guarding the cave?" I asked. "And what is Genesis Time?"

She laughed, and instead of answering, kissed me. "There is so much I will have to teach you," she murmured, equivocally. "Perhaps it will be better if I explain things as they happen." She motioned with one hand toward a smallish brown building in front of which our cars had stopped.

The guards remained in the tricars, while Lyagin, Yasi, and I went up three stairs to the house. A woman waited for us at the door. She was a tall woman, with a corded, austere body, and nearly as old as Lyagin.

She led us to a large interior room, with a single round window, and walls hung with beautiful furs of many colors. She took a seat on a blue, divan-like chair, and sat in quiet repose, with her hands folded in her lap.

Yasi put an arm in mine and led me to one side of the room. "We are to be only witnesses," she whispered. "The formality of courtship is about to begin."

Lyagin put down a carrying case he had brought into the room, and reached inside and brought out a small doll and brought it over to the woman. She refused it, turning her head with an expression of high hauteur.

Lyagin put the doll on the floor and returned to his bag and took out a folded piece of cloth, that was apparently a scarf. The woman refused that also, and Lyagin brought her a small object that resembled a pincushion.

The woman regarded the object doubtfully, but allowed Lyagin to place it in her lap. He went into the next room then, and came out a few minutes later with a bowl of some kind of soup. When he knelt on one knee and offered her a spoonful, the woman accepted, and allowed him to feed her several more—and the symbolic courtship was over.

We went on to a larger apartment building then, dropping Lyagin and the mem-mother at one apartment, and going on to the one next door. To the "cave."

The cave consisted of one room, without windows and sparsely furnished.

I did not have time to inspect it immediately, however, for another urgent matter intruded as soon as the door was closed—and locked—behind us. Yasi had put both arms around my neck, and kissed me, with great urgency. We stayed embraced, and eased to the floor, where we loved again, as passionately as before, and at the end lay on the floor, face to face, breathing in each other's breath, both completely lost in awe of the depth of the love that bound us.

Several minutes later Yasi began undressing me—and I her. We lay together then, letting the warmth of our bodies produce an alchemy that revived our briefly sated energies. Yasi kissed me all over my body, and afterward I held her close, reveling in every charm cradled so tightly against me, and breathing in her delicate, stimulating msst.

Until I could restrain myself no longer, and I entered her again. This time we had no haste to spend our passion. That had been lessened by the early vigor and fury of our loving, and now the orifices of love were not so replete that the finish couldn't be postponed.

I pressed myself on her until the fierce lovelight in her eyes dulled to a glaze of contentment, and I rested, with my cheek on the soft woman flesh of her chest.

For two hours we lay in our love immersion, moving only enough to reawaken our love sensations when they dulled, often changing positions, sometimes on our sides, and sometimes with Yasi above.

Once, we heard the heavy beating of raindrops on our roof, and a crash of thunder that rolled across the sky. We disregarded them, knowing that nature was nurturing a thunderstorm here within our cave that would surpass the one outside.

At the end, near the last of the third hour, Yasi reached a point where she could no longer contain the fiery ebb and flow of turbulence within, and her movements grew abruptly fierce and demanding, and I responded, and an instant later we were caught up in a colossal, incredible, exploding nova!

I had the absolute conviction that never before had any man and woman, Human or Veldqan, ever reached that peak of passionate ecstasy.

Yasi dropped swiftly to sleep then, while I lay for many long minutes contemplating the wonder of woman, this one in particular. She opened her eyes then, and kissed me idly, and I lay on my back and contemplated the near-bare room around us. "This is the cave?" I took the belated opportunity to ask.

She smiled. "The pseudo cave, of course. In ancient times the couple to be married were brought up the mountain to a cave by the girl's parents. After they entered, the parents closed the mouth of the cave with boulders, and guarded the honeymooning couple against dangers. Usually there was none, for the cave was always higher up than the dleeth ventured, and the violating of a Genesis cave by rival clansmen was a crime punished by instant death—without even the honor of the Final Game.

The shadow of death that had been hanging over me for so long had diminished during the past days, but it returned then and I found myself a bit annoyed with Yasi. Even she considered the Final Game a death with honor. She would probably watch me undergo it more with pride than sorrow, I thought peevishly, knowing even while I thought it that I was being unjustly harsh with her. These people, were different, it appeared, by most every standard I possessed.

Yasi was so finely attuned to me by this time, that though I gave no sign, she read that I was disturbed, and she turned to me and said, "You will be fruitful. I would lay my life on it." In her tone was a touch of fear.

Which gave birth to another puzzle.

"Our room is sealed, as immutably as if it were actually a cave on the mountainside, with boulders in front," she stated. "We will not leave here until I am pregnant—or one of us is dead."

Her words cleared up very little, but I was patient, knowing that she would explain in her own way.

"You see, we have been left with no food," she continued, her voice troubled. "You will make me pregnant, or our hunger will grow greater, until one of us dies." She paused and regarded me speculatively, sadly. "The man will always die first," she said, "for we women have our accumulated flesh, that will nourish us in our need." She cried then, with her cheek against mine, and exclaimed through her tears, "We cannot let ourselves fail!"

The Veldqan survival ethos again. The nonproductive male

would be eliminated, while the woman would survive—to be able still to foster the race. I doubt that the custom would have originated if it were the woman who died first. Another of their mores, I reflected, no longer functional, but clung to adamantly.

I held Yasi close, until her anxiety lessened, while I asked myself if the discoveries here would ever cease. I weighed, with some apprehension, my chances. Two different races, with the probability against a successful mating so great as to be considered impossible—except that Darlene and Trobt had demonstrated otherwise. Had that been an anomaly, I wondered, or an accident of nature?

I would soon learn. Probably to my sorrow.

All that day and the next Yasi spent in a covert chase. She seemed to have an insatiable craving for being loved, and she observed me, talked with me and to me, and teased me, always alert to take advantage of every moment when I might be able to respond to her.

I was never certain whether nature had implanted that lusty appetite, or if her concern for my life occasioned the greater part of her ardor. All I knew is that we loved on every clear space and corner of our small dwelling, and in every imaginable way. Until the third day, when I felt that I had no iota of love left to give her.

By that time my appetite had passed from hunger to craving for great quantities of food, and finally to apathy. I could not possibly be starving in that short time, but I felt as though the flesh were shrinking from my bones, that I had grown old and weak. I had to realize that more than hunger had weakened me, but my spirits failed to revive. I knew that I would die there.

And then it came!

Yasi had lured me to her bed again, and tried to resurrect my confidence by taking a hand and pressing it over a fulsome breast, when suddenly she gave a cry of joy. "It is here!" The words gushed out.

She placed my hand that she had been holding against her stomach. "Feel," she commanded. "Here. And here. And here." She moved my hand about her middle. "The Genesis!" she squealed, wrapping both arms and legs about me in a semi-crushing embrace.

In each place she put my hand I had felt a subtle stirring, as though small rivers were flowing beneath the skin. This was evidently the sign for which she had been waiting.

I returned her fierce hug, wondering with one portion of my mind at the inner workings of this so familiar but alien girl. Certainly they must have only small resemblance to those of a Human female.

Yasi and I celebrated our triumph one more time, in the best way, in the same way we had been celebrating our marriage, and afterward she went to the door and pounded on it, and shouted, in a happy boisterous way, "It is here! It is here!"

The door opened.

Our honeymoon was not yet over, I soon learned. The first three days had actually been the cave or Genesis Time, the honeymoon would be spent in a more elaborate setting, and at a more leisurely pace—as I also learned.

Lyagin had kept a personal car waiting for us, and we boarded it when we left our cave, with Yasi driving. I still had not tried the cars, and saw little reason for doing so. I was skeptical of my ability to drive one.

Yasi drove with all the verve and dash of a racing driver, wheeling us through the city, past pedestrians and other tricars, with never a hint of hesitation, until we reached a gate in the wall and went out.

We drove across the red sand and the grassland, to the same mountain, with its white sides, that I had observed in my truck-train ride to the Veldq factories. The trip was much quicker than before. I judged the cruising speed of the tricar at about thirty-five miles an hour, while the trains—still transporting their machinery on the tracks beside us—moved at about ten miles an hour.

We reached the mountain and followed a trail up the side for perhaps three miles before coming to our destination: a square, one-story log structure that must have measured a hundred feet on a side.

The huge cabin was unlocked and we went inside—and I

witnessed the nearest thing to a luxury dwelling that I had seen on Veldq. The Veldqans must place considerable stress on the happiness of the newlyweds. It was composed of eight spacious rooms, all elaborately furnished, with walls hung with ornamental furs and woven fabrics. Nowhere had I seen a picture, however, in the cabin or any other place in Hearth. There again they differed from our Worlds.

Another difference, a personal one, I noted when Yasi led me all about the house, inspecting it, and everything in it, before she led me to a fur-covered bench in an outdoor garden, and we finally made love. I learned then that though her ardor had cooled somewhat, had become less urgent and more placid, it was just as wonderful.

We finished, and sat up on the bench, and I gazed about me. The trees and shrubbery were all carefully tendered, I noted. Gardeners must have left shortly before we arrived. A small waterfall splashing at one end of the garden had been formed by turning a natural stream over a rock ledge and into the grounds, and channeled to flow through. It contributed to a beautiful landscape.

We spent the day lounging about the house and grounds, resting as would runners who had completed a long enervating marathon—which figuratively we had—and I slept ten long hours that night.

I would have been content lounging through another day, but Yasi, who had been the first to rise, had prepared a breakfast of some small animal, that she had baked to an appetizing brown, and a celery-like vegetable, which despite its shape tasted like a sweet potato. The meal was delicious, spiced by the fresh air we had experienced the day before, and my many hours of sleep.

Yasi became restless shortly after our meal, and when I saw her bring out thicker and warmer cloaks than those we had brought with us, I knew she planned a trip.

We each carried a pack and a pair of snowshoes much like those of Earth when we started out, and I had no difficulty in guessing that we were heading for a snow field I could see a couple of miles up the trail.

We hadn't gone far before I began breathing deeply. The air was thinner here, and the gravity seemed as heavy, and my stamina was not great. Yasi allowed me to rest often, but otherwise pressed steadily forward.

At the end of an hour we reached the snow field, but paused only long enough to put on our snowshoes. We trudged upward then until we reached a plain with a wide expanse of virgin snow.

Yasi must have been looking for such a spot, for she kicked off her snowshoes then, spread her cloak on a bank of snow, and lay on it. I needed only the look in her eyes to understand what was expected of me. As the old quip goes—I didn't even take off my skis. (Snowshoes.)

We ate afterward, cold slices of the animal we had eaten partly for breakfast, and squares of flat bread.

We loved one more time, on the way down, this time on the very edge of a precipice. We had taken a different trail, one we could never have managed on the way up, for we had to break our way through soft snow with a hard crust that would not bear our weight.

When we came to the precipice I made ready to skirt it when I saw Yasi spread her cloak again—with a dare in her eyes. I accepted, and loved her with a thousand feet of bare rock staring at me from a mere six inches away. I was very careful not to loosen the snow beneath us—lest we fall that thousand feet.

Here was that Veldq daring again, this time in my own sweet Yasi, I reflected even as we had our joy, the love of danger, of tempting fate, the playing of a gambler's hand, and being prepared to take the consequences if one lost. As delightful as loving Yasi was, I'm not certain I approved of our taking such risks.

As we continued our downhill trek I made a point to look for signs of animal life. I quickly spotted balls of thick rich fur on the trees, about the size of house cats, and watching them, saw occasional bits of bark drop to the ground. They were quite plentiful, and I guessed that they furnished most of the furs the Veldqans used so lavishly.

Once a predator, a weasel-like animal half the size of the bark-eaters, appeared suddenly and sank a long thin appendage on its nose into one of the fur balls. It offered no resistance, remaining motionless, while—I supposed—the weasel drained its fill of blood. I saw no other animals except a group of many-legged herbivores, that Yasi pointed out on a ledge far below us.

"Are there no—" I began, as we moved on, but could find no Veldqan word for birds. "Do you have small animals that" (no precise word for fly, so I tried substituting hand flappings) "through the air?" I never did get her to understand what I meant.

We stayed on the mountain for eight days, and our honeymoon was over. That much I regretted, but I was eager to return to Hearth. In my mind a small tentative tide was flowing—like the small tides in Yasi's stomach.

I knew the feeling well. The annotator. It had gathered most of the facts it needed for some momentous conclusion. Perhaps days would go by, perhaps only hours, until some final observation or idea would be gathered—and I would have the answer. Perhaps *the* answer this time. If I could be alone for a period. . . .

Back in Hearth we spent a day riding and driving, as happy as only newly-marrieds could be, until near the end of the day, when we climbed the stairs of a building I had not heard named—the next highest to the Games Building in the City—and stood looking out over Hearth, with wind and the first flakes of a rising storm in our faces, when it came to me. . . .

I had the answer to all that I had come to Veldq to find!

I had been noting the high wall about Hearth, and as I idly speculated on whether the primitive devices used in the days of Earth's knighthood could have breached it, my thoughts switched to the great wall of China. And. . . .

CHINA!!!

The annotator gave its almost audible click, and the answer lay in my hands, a gift waiting to be opened.

I quickly banished the wonder of it, resolved at that moment to do nothing about it for the time being—Yasi and I had to have more time to ourselves.

* * *

However, I was able only to restrain myself for two more days, and I kissed Yasi for what might have been the last time, and set out for Trobt's office.

I found him working at his semi-circular table.

"One question," I said, after our preliminary greetings. "Do you still regard war between Veldq and the Federation as inevitable?"

"It cannot be otherwise."

I could not contradict that. "Do you remember telling me that if I knew of any way to lessen the havoc and bloodshed I should tell you?" I asked.

"Certainly."

My next words, I knew, would shock him. "I'm going to ask you to allow me to return to our Worlds," I said. "I am going to recommend unconditional surrender."

Trobt regarded me as though I had spoken gibberish. "Can you be serious?" he asked finally.

"I am very serious," I answered him.

His face grew gaunt almost as though he were making the surrender rather than I. I detected a touch of scorn. "Is this decision dictated by your logic," he asked dryly, "or by faintness of heart?"

I did not honor the question with an answer, though I understood his view of it very well.

Trobt did not apologize. "You understand that unconditional surrender is the only kind we will accept?" he asked.

I nodded wearily.

"Will they agree to your recommendation?"

"No," I answered. "Humans are not cowards, and they will fight—as long as there is any slightest chance of success. I will not be able to convince them that defeat is inevitable. However, I can prepare them for what is to come. I hope to shorten the conflict immeasurably."

"I can do nothing but accept," Trobt said, after a moment of thought. "One does not kick a dog lying on its back." He made his opinion of me plain with his tone as well as with his words. I became uncomfortably warm, but made no attempt to defend myself.

"I will arrange transportation back to Earth for you tomorrow," Trobt said. I had to admire that rapid decision, he had never given me cause to think I had overestimated him at our first meeting. He regarded me with expressionless eyes, and cut me one more time. "You realize that an enemy who surrenders without a struggle is beneath contempt?" he asked, hoping, I guessed, that I'd fight back.

I had lost him completely now. The warmth in my body forced its flush into my cheeks, but I made an all-out effort to ignore his taunt, and succeeded, barely. "Will you give me six months before you move against us?" I asked. "The Federation is large. I will need time to bring my message to all."

"You have your six months." Trobt was still not through with me, personally. "On the exact day that period ends I will expect you back on Veldq. We will see if you have any honor left."

"I'll be back," I told him, without bluster.

Before I made my return to Earth known I bought a small farm near the Porcupine Mountains in Michigan's upper peninsula—under an assumed name. Before too long I would be regarded as a traitor by most of the Ten Thousand Worlds. And as a live coward, when I might better have been a dead hero.

I had just enough influence with the politicos—and they enough curiosity—to arrange a meeting with delegates from our sector of the Worlds. I presented them with what I had learned, and recommended unconditional surrender.

They laughed at me. These men were all descendants of pioneer stock, their nature was to fight—until it had been proven to them incontrovertibly, that they could not win. Words would never do it.

However, I had expected as much. I gave them all the arguments I had, then moved on to the other Worlds and presented them with the same message.

The reaction was identical everywhere. No surrender. They were only convinced that they must make hasty preparations to fight. Still I continued my mission. Wherever possible I induced them to telecast our talks, so that as many people as possible could learn what I had to say. I covered as much territory as I was physically able to in the first five months.

The last month I saved for the Jason's Fleece sector. They

were the Worlds nearest the Veldqans, and would be first to bleed in the coming conflict. They evidenced the greatest unease—a few delegates vacillated—but in the end all refused to take my recommendations at face value.

The last day I returned to Veldq.

12

Trobt received me with no sign of our former friendship. There was no man I'd known whose respect I valued more, yet there was nothing I could do to recover his good regard. I suspected that I had lost it forever.

An hour after my return I paid a visit to Yondtl. I did not go to Yasi first, for I knew that if I did I wouldn't be able to leave.

I had seldom been consciously aware of my intention to challenge Yondtl again, but I'm certain the annotator pondered it often. For I was not entirely convinced that he was the better man. My familiarity with the Game had been only brief, while he had played for many years. It had hardly been a fair test.

I had engaged in only a few Games since the first match with Yondtl, but whenever some new aspect or strategy came to mind I gave it my best analysis, then consigned it to the annotator—where it would be thoroughly digested. I would engage him again with little evidence of my earlier neophyte play.

When I greeted Yondtl I was mildly surprised to hear him speak—even though it was only a few brief words, or perhaps grunts would describe them better. "Welcome—friend—" And I found myself deeply touched to see the sincerity he put into the "friend." Our contests had evidently endeared me to him.

Yondtl's mother served as his hands. The first Game I played carefully, cautiously—and gained only a tie.

For the second I threw everything at him that I had absorbed during the past few months.

He won.

He won the next also.

So much for that.

I returned to Yasi then. My hunger for her was still as great as on our honeymoon—engaging all the capacity of my emotional makeup.

This time my stay with her was brief. Veldq's Council acted two days after my return. They were going to give the Humans no more time to organize counteraction. The six months they had already granted could be considered evidence of a great sense of fair play—or of great confidence in their own strength.

I went in the same spaceship that carried Trobt; I intended to give him any advice he needed about the Worlds. I asked in return only that his first stops be at the Jason's Fleece fringe.

Beside us sailed a mighty armada of warships, spaced in a long line that would encompass the entire portion of the galaxy occupied by the Fleece Worlds. For an hour we moved ponderously forward, then the stars about us winked out for an instant. The next moment a group of Worlds became visible on the ship's vision screen. I recognized them as Jason's Fleece.

One world expanded until it became the size of a baseball. "Quagman," Trobt said.

Quagman, the trouble spot of the Ten Thousand Worlds. Dominated by an unscrupulous clique that ruled by vendetta, it had been the source of much trouble and vexation to the other Worlds. Its leaders were considered little better than brigands. They had received me with much apparent courtesy, and in the end they had even agreed to surrender to the Veldqans—when and if they appeared. I had accepted their facile concurrence uneasily, but they were my principal hope.

Two Veldqans left the ship in a scooter. We waited. Few words were spoken. Trobt played with the child's ring on his belt, a favorite ornament of the Veldqans, reminiscent of the time of the dleeth. He still spoke to me only when necessary. All our empathy had disappeared the day I made our offer of surrender.

At the end of ten long, tense hours word came from the Quagmans, through instruments on the Veldqan ship that I had adjusted to receive them. The two messengers were being held for ransom. They would be released upon the delivery of two billion dollars—in the currency of any recognized World—or its equivalence in precious stones or metals. And the promise of immunity from attack.

The fools!

Trobt's face remained impassive as he read the message aloud. Mine, I'm certain, blanched.

We waited several more hours. Both Trobt and I glanced often at the green, mottled baseball on the vision screen. It was Trobt who first pointed out a small, barely discernible black spot on the upper right rim of Quagman.

As the hours passed, and the black spot swung slowly to the left as the planet revolved, it grew almost imperceptibly larger. When it disappeared over the edge of the World we retired. I did not sleep.

In the morning the spot appeared again, and now it covered nearly half the face of the planet. Another ten hours and the entire World became a blackened cinder.

Quagman was dead.

The ship moved next to Mican.

Mican was a sparsely populated prison planet. Criminals were usually sent to newly discovered Worlds on the edge of Human expansion and allowed to make their own attempts at achieving a stable government. Men with restless natures which often made them criminals on their own highly civilized Worlds, as often made them excellent pioneers. However, it always took them several generations to work their way up from anarchy to cooperative government. Mican had not yet had that time. I had done my best in the week I spent there to convince the Micanians to organize, and to be prepared to accept any terms the Veldqans offered. The effort, I feared, was in vain, but I had given all the arguments I knew. At the end I decided they had to be the second World visited by the Veldqans, a most difficult judgment.

A scooter left with two Veldqan representatives. When it returned Trobt left the control room to speak with them.

He came back to where I waited, shaking his head. It would have been useless for me to argue.

Mican died.

At my request Trobt agreed to give the remaining Jason's Fleece Worlds a week to consider—on the condition that they make no offensive forays. I wanted them to have time to assess fully what had happened to the other two Worlds—to realize that that stubbornness would result in the same disaster for them. God give them the wisdom to agree, I prayed.

At the end of the third twenty-four-hour period the Jason's Fleece Worlds surrendered—unconditionally. They had tasted blood and recognized futility when faced with it. That had been the best I had been able to hope for, earlier.

Each sector held off surrendering until the one immediately ahead had given in. But at the end the capitulation was complete. No more blood had to be shed.

The Veldqans' terms left the Worlds definitely subservient, but they were neither unnecessarily harsh nor humiliating. Veldq demanded specific limitations on weapons and war-making potentials. (Which, incidentally, proved to be good for the Worlds: there was less bickering, and no more sporadic military engagements between the Worlds, and their internal order was better.) The Veldqans also imposed the obligation of reporting all technological and scientific progress, and colonial expansion was permitted only by prior consent.

There was little actual occupation of Federation Worlds, but the Veldqans retained the right to inspect any and all functions of the various governments. Other aspects of social and economic methods would be subject only to occasional checks and investigation. Projects considered questionable would be supervised by the Veldqans at their own discretion.

The one provision that caused any vigorous protest from the Worlds was the Veldqan demand for Human women. But even that was a purely emotional reaction, and died as soon as it was more fully understood.

The Veldqans were not savages. They used no coercion to obtain their mates. They demanded only the same right to woo the women as the Human males had. No woman would be taken without her free choice. There could be no valid protest to that. Especially as demand was abetted by the unexpectedly cheerful acquiescence of the women.

In practice it worked quite well. On nearly all the Worlds there were more women than men, so that few men had to go without mates because of the Veldqan inroads. And—by Human standards—they seldom took our most desireable women. Because Veldqan women gained weight as they became sexually responsive, their men had an almost universal preference for fleshy women. As a result many of our women who would have had difficulty securing Human husbands found themselves much in demand as mates of the Veldqans.

One other result, unforeseen, but quite normal when considered: The women chosen by the Veldqans soon developed a class-conscious, superior, attitude. They were the wives of the rulers, and many of them looked down on the Worlds' women as aristocrats would look with condescension on commoners. Human nature?

Eight years passed after the Worlds' capitulation before I saw Kalin Trobt again.

The pact between the Veldqans and the Federation had worked out well, for both sides. The demands of the Veldqans entailed little sacrifice by the Federation, and the necessity of reporting to a superior authority made for less wrangling and jockeying for trade and other advantages among the Worlds themselves.

The fact that the Veldqans had taken more than twenty million of our women—it was the custom of the Veldqan males to take one, but no more than one, Human woman for a mate—caused little dislocation or discontent. The number lost did far less than balance the Human ratio of the sexes.

For the Veldqans the pace solved the warrior-set frustrations, and the unrest and sexual starvation of their males. All could now obtain mates whose biological makeup did not necessitate an eight-to-one ratio. Those men who demanded action and adventure were given supervisory posts on the Worlds as an outlet for their drives, a quite excellent sublimation.

Each year it became easier for the Humans to understand the Veldqans, and to meet them on common grounds socially. In turn, the Veldqans' nature became less rigid, and they laughed more—even at themselves, when the occasion warranted.

This was noticeable especially among the younger Veldqans, just reaching an adult status. In later years when the majority would have a mixture of Human blood, the differences between us would become less pronounced.

How Trobt found me I did not learn. I was still living under my assumed name. The rancor that had accompanied the name of Leonard Stromberg through the early years of peace had almost died out now. However, I had come to enjoy my isolation in the Porcupine Mountains, and I had made no effort to return to my former friends and associates.

Trobt made his appearance as I was weeding my garden. He had changed very little during those eight years. His hair had grayed some at the temples and his movements were a bit less supple but he looked well. Much of the intensity had left his aquiline features, and he too seemed content.

We shook hands with very real pleasure. I led him to chairs under the shade of a nearby tree and poured lemonade for both of us.

Yasi heard him from the kitchen and came out and they embraced warmly. "I see that there will be a second spring this year," Trobt quipped, referring to the embryo evidence of the coming of Yasi's second fertile period. It was the first time I had heard the semblance of a conscious joke from that quarter.

Yasi laughed with him. "Soon I will be taking Leonard to the cave," she answered. I gave a mock shudder, and she inquired about the health of Yondtl, and was told that he was very happy with his new limbs, and could speak as well now as any Veldqan. Human surgical techniques had been very welcome there.

Yondtl had taken to writing lately, Trobt informed us. "Quite weighty tomes, I believe," he said.

Yasi went to the edge of the valley that bordered the garden,

Outstanding science fiction and fantasy

Presenting MICHAEL MOORCOCK
in DAW editions

The Elric Novels

and called down, and a few minutes later our son emerged from a copse of woods and came running up to the house.

I have always felt that I was justified in having more than a father's normal pride in him. He was a serious student, even at his early age, straightforward in character and in thought, and always courteous. Mainly the result of Yasi's upbringing, I conceded. There was a close personal relationship between the two, so much so that sometimes I wondered if I might not be the outsider here. Yet I knew better, the boy had my sense of humor, and eagerness for knowledge, and both he and his mother loved me dearly, I was certain.

"I would like you to meet my son, Kalin." I introduced him to Trobt and watched his eyes light with pleasure. I saw then that our old empathy had returned, and that I had pleased him greatly by naming my son after him.

The two Kalins shook hands solemnly. "He has my stern brows," Trobt remarked, with a small attempt at Earthian face-tiousness. We all laughed more heartily than the jest warranted, but that was because of the great conviviality of the occasion.

Soon young Kalin returned to his place of play, and Yasi to her kitchen, and Trobt and I were left alone. We sat for many long minutes, content simply with our great rapport.

Until Trobt said, "I want to apologize for having thought you a coward. I know now how very wrong I was. When you played the Game your forte was finding the weakness of an opponent. And winning the second game. You made no attempt to win the first. I see now, that as on the boards, your surrender represented only the conclusion of the first game, where you sought our weakness. You found that weakness, and were confident that there would be a second game, and that you would use it against us. And that your Ten Thousand Worlds would win. He drew in his breath, and let it out in a sigh. "As you have won," he said.

"What would you say that weakness was?" By now I suspected that he knew everything, but I wanted to be certain so as not to say anything that would offend him.

"Our desire and need for Human women, of course."

There was no need to dissemble further. "The solution came to me first," I explained, "when I remembered a formerly independent Earth country named China. They lost most of their wars, but in the end they always won."

"Through their women?"

"Indirectly. Actually it was done by absorbing their conquerors. Conquerors are seldom able to bring many of their women with them, and are forced to intermarry with the vanquished people. The Chinese always greatly outnumbered their victors, and intermarriage quickly prevailed in all instances, with the inevitable result that in time the conquering races disappeared.

"The situation was similar with Veldq and the Ten Thousand Worlds. Veldq won the war, but in a thousand years there will be no Veldqans, racially."

"That was my first realization," Trobt said. "I saw immediately then how you had us hopelessly trapped. The marriage of our men to your women will merge our bloods until—with your vastly greater numbers—in a dozen generations there will be only traces of our race left.

"And what can we do about it?" Trobt continued, with apparent resignation. "We can't kill our beloved wives—and our children. We can't stop further acquisition of Human women without disrupting our society. With each generation the tie between us will become closer, our blood thinner, yours more dominant, as the intermingling continues. We cannot even declare war against the people who are doing this to us. How do you fight an enemy who has surrendered unconditionally?"

"You understand that for your side it was the only solution to the imminent chaos that faced you?" I asked.

"Yes, I suppose so." I watched Trobt's swift mind go through its reasoning. I was certain he saw that Veldq was losing only an arbitrary distinction of race, very similar to the absorbing of the early clans of Veldq into the family of the Danlee. Their dislike of that was definitely only an emotional consideration. The blending of our bloods would benefit both, and the resultant race would be better and stronger because of the blending.

With a small smile Trobt raised his glass. "We will drink to the union of two great races," he toasted.

"And to you—the winner of the Second Game!"

Outstanding science fiction and fantasy